Norse Mythology

Explore the Timeless Tales of Norse Folklore, the Myths, History, Sagas & Legends of the Gods, Immortals, Magical Creatures, Vikings & More

Sofia Visconti

Subscribe To Sofia Visconti

As a subscriber you will receive a _Free Gift_ + You wil be the first to hear about new books, articles and more exclusives **just for you**

Click Here

Table of Contents

Introduction

The first world that came into existence, before the beginning of time, was Muspelheim, a realm of fire, flames, and heat. To the north lay the realm of ice and frost, Niflheim, and separating the two contrasting lands was Ginnungagap, the world of chaos, a great abyss of void and nothingness. But, as Ginnungagap met both the world of ice and the land of flames, it linked the two. The venomous waters of Niflheim flew into the void, stuck in a perpetual cycle of freezing and thawing caused by the hot winds that blew into the vast nothingness from Muspelheim. The water drops that came from the union of the two natural elements, ice, and fire, built up and took the form of the frost giant Ymir, the first of his kind and the earliest form of life in Nordic mythology.

The birth of Ymir marks the beginning of the mythical world of the Nordic people, and it paves the way for all the myths and legends that are to come; stories of the clever and driven Odin, of the courageous Thor and devious Loki, characters that we are all more or less accustomed to. Lately, the fascination with the Vikings, their beliefs, and their way of life is at its peak. We see mythological Norse heroes and gods in popular movies, we have TV shows starring fearless Vikings and their historical conquests, and we have comics and video games that allow us to follow along with the adventures and legends of the old Nords.

And yet, all these mediums take artistic liberties, and at the end of the day, we are left striving for more. We want to get to know the people behind the fantastic stories. We want to understand where these legends are coming from and what they meant for the Nordic civilization. This desire to learn more and understand the culture that created the gods and heroes we love, and to discover characters, creatures, and legends that didn't get the "media treatment" they deserved, needs an outlet. I hope that this book can become yours.

I am Sofia Visconti, a mythology expert, and an Amazon bestselling author. I can wholeheartedly say that the success of my books comes solely from my passion for the subject. I'm an absolute mythology freak, and there's nothing I love more than introducing people to the wonderful world of gods, legends, and breathtaking creatures. What makes mythology so fascinating is not the stories in themselves, although some are truly a feast to the eyes, but how they came to be and what they mean for the people that live by them. Mythology is nothing more than a creative expression of a culture. It embodies the beliefs, way of life, and values of a civilization, representing its identity. That is why each mythology is unique, and it can't exist apart from its culture. This also applies to Norse mythology. To understand it on a deeper level and connect with it, we must first get to know the Nords and how they saw the world they lived in. I can't wait to go on this adventure with you and show you the great and exciting world of the Vikings!

By the end of this book, you will be more familiarized with the gods and legends of Norse mythology, as well as the people who created them. You'll know who the Norse were, how they lived their lives, their beliefs, their faith as a civilization, and how they influenced the modern world. And, of course, you'll know more about your favorite gods, such as how Odin became the ruler of the Aesir gods, how Thor got his famous hammer Mjolnir, and who Loki's children are. I hope that the magical creatures of the Norse world and the peculiar characters of the Nordic tales will conquer your heart as it did mine!

Now before we start, if you're a beginner into the endeavors of mythology, there is something you should keep in mind: expect the unexpected and don't be discouraged when things appear to not make sense. I admit that most stories tend to be quite weird or have mystifying elements. Take that as part of the old' mythology charm and don't dwell too much on the unexplainable. I will do my best to analyze the myths and explain their origins and meanings, but not everything has scientific answers, and that's ok.

Another thing to keep in mind is that Nordic gods and heroes are not perfect beings. They have human characteristics, making them charmingly flawed. They get angry, make mistakes, act on the spur of the moment, and can be very cruel at times. However, that is what makes the Norse gods so appealing. We can relate to them and connect with them on a deeper level. They don't represent untouchable standards. That's why the Norse people were so close with their gods and saw them as role models as well as fearful forces subjected to whims and tempers.

With everything out of the way, let's imagine ourselves following into the steps of the great Odin. He sought knowledge, and in order to get it, he was willing to sacrifice anything. And so he did, by handing himself from Yggdrasill, the tree of life, to get the runes of knowledge, and by giving up one of his eyes to drink from the Well of Knowledge. Odin's hunger for wisdom is evident in many of the stories that involve him, and I invite you to share his willingness to let go of your reality and jump into the mysterious world of the old Norse.

Let's drink from the Well of Knowledge and jump into a realm of wonder, where nothing is as it seems!

Chapter 1: A Brief History of the Norseman

The Norse people, commonly known as Vikings, were seafaring warlords and warriors from the pagan Scandinavia. They had such a great impact on Europe's history that the time in which they raided, colonized, and conquered European soils, from around the ninth to the 11th century, was named after them: "the Viking Age." When we hear the word "Vikings" we can't help but imagine an army of barbarians who bowed to no gods and who only took pleasure in plundering and raiding. Honestly, we are not to blame for having this mental image. That's just how Vikings are usually portrayed, and the concept is stuck somewhere deep in our subconscious mind. But is this image close to the historical truth? Let's see!

The Origins of Vikings

Vikings came from Sweden, Norway, and Denmark, many hundreds of years before they were recognized as stand-alone countries, and they were mostly land-owning farmers and fishermen. They lived in villages ruled by chieftains or clan leaders, and they had few towns. Chieftains often fought for dominance over the lands, and with a seemingly inexhaustible arsenal of strong men who sought adventure, it was fairly easy for skillful leaders to organize armies and fearful bands. Historians are unsure what prompted Vikings to leave their lands and become seafaring pillagers, but they do propose a couple of theories.

The political instability caused by the frequent clashes between clans makes a good motive for branching out. Another would be localized overpopulation, which led to families owning smaller and smaller lands that could no longer provide sustenance for all the family members.

Additionally, around the seventh and eighth centuries, the Vikings refined the way they constructed ships and vessels, adding sails and modifying their structures to sustain longer voyages. These longships were swift and shallow, allowing them to go across the North Sea and land on the beaches of unsuspecting lands. If we consider shipping advances, the troubled socio-economic situation of the Vikings at the time, the adventurous nature of these warrior-spirited people, and the tales of riches brought along by merchants, it's not hard to understand why one day they decided to raid the coasts of Europe.

The Start of the Viking Era

The first historical account of a Viking classical hit-and-run raid dates back to the year 793, when a monastery in Lindisfarne, England was plundered of its sacred, golden religious artifacts. Though, as a side note here, it is unlikely that this was the first time the Vikings attacked England.

Evidence shows that English coastal villages had started to organize defenses against sea attacks earlier in the eighth century, suggesting that there were Viking raids or at least attempts before the attack on the Lindisfarne monastery. Many medieval English documents refer to them as "seagoing pagans" for their tendency to target holy places, which, to be fair, were full of unarmed men and gold, so who can blame the Vikings for taking the opportunity? The term "Viking," which is derived from the old Scandinavian word *vikingir* (pirate) or from the word *vik,* which means "bay," was popularized closer to the end of the historical Viking Age. Terms such as *Dani* (inhabitants of present Denmark), *Normani* (Northmen), and simply *pagani* (pagans) were more generally used when referring to the Scandinavian warriors by the European people who were unlucky enough to face their wrath.

From the year 793 forwards, Viking bands consisting of freemen, retainers, and young, adventure-seeking men led by chieftains had gone on to further attack England and its surroundings, especially Scotland, Ireland, and France. Additionally, some accounts from the latter years of the Viking Era speak of Viking attacks or sightings in the Iberian Peninsula, Ukraine, Russia, and even the Byzantine Empire. Originally, the raids were pretty small-scale. There were only a handful of ships, and the Vikings would happily return home when they collected enough booty or if they encountered a resilient defense. But from the 850s, the Vikings began to double down on the force and organization of their raids, establishing bases in the newly conquered lands and starting to dominate the surrounding island areas.

Viking Raids in England and Scotland

In 865, England was struck by the *micel here* (the great army) of Ivar the Boneless and Haldfan, a pair of brothers and the sons of Ragnar Lothbrok - a renowned Viking warrior. They attacked the

Anglo-Saxon kingdoms one-by-one, capturing the ancient kingdoms of Northumbria, Eastern Anglia, and most of the kingdom of Mercia. By the year 878, only Wessex, a southern kingdom led by the inexperienced King Alfred, was standing. In January of that year, the Viking forces led by Guthrum attacked Alfred by surprise at his royal estate in Chippenham. The king of Wessex barely made it out alive, but he managed to gather an army and defeat Guthrum at Edington.

Despite Alfred's victory, most of England was controlled by Vikings. They held the north and the Midlands, and for the next 80 years, the territory remained divided between Alfred's successors and Viking kings. Eirik Bloodaxe, the last Viking ruler of England, was killed by Eadred, King Alfred's grandson, in 954, putting an end to the Viking control and uniting England. Other Viking attempts at reconquering England were only briefly successful, with England being for a while part of the empire of Canute, another Scandinavian king. In 1042, England's Viking Era ended, with the restoration of its native ruler, William I. Although no longer under Viking control, the seafaring warriors left deep marks on the area, influencing the social structure, dialects, and customs of England. Fun fact, William's great-great-great-grandfather was Rollo, a Viking. So, the Viking influence over England goes deeper than we might imagine.

Scotland was struck in 794, and the Vikings took control of the Hebrides, Shetlands, and the Orkneys. Their hold on Scotland was long-lasting, and they remained in control of Orkneys well into the 11th century.

Western Dominance

In the west, the Viking expansion was ruthless. They invaded Iceland, Greenland, and they even attempted to settle in North America (which they called *Vinland,* a name that roughly translates to "the land of wild grapes"). The Norse saga "*Eirik the Red's Saga*" credits Leif, son of Eirik the Red, as the accidental discoverer of North America, while "*The Saga of the Greenlanders*" claims that Bjarni Herjolfsson, a Viking explorer, was the first to lay eyes on Vinland. Although we can't know for sure who the Scandinavian Columbus was, we do know that Vikings made it to North America, thanks to the discovery of the L'Anse aux Meadows archeological site. The archeological remains of ancient houses were found in the 1960s by Helge Instad, a Norwegian explorer, and his wife Anne Stine, an archeologist. Although the site is unlikely to have housed the main Vinland colony, it still confirms the epic Viking sagas.

Viking raids in Ireland began around the year 795, and, despite valiant resistance from the natives, the Vikings managed to establish kingdoms and fortified ports. Waterford, Limerick, and Dublin were under Scandinavian control, and in 1014 there was a failed attempt to unify Ireland under the Scandinavian rule. Even so, the Vikings remained dominant even early into the 12th century, when the English invasion started.

Viking Attacks on France and the End of the Viking Age

Viking raids on France started a bit later, in 799, and the Scandinavian powers benefited a lot from the political turmoils of the Frankish kingdom. Their powers grew exponentially, and in 885, they almost conquered Paris. However, the Carolingian empire was too great of a foe for a nation of raiders and pillagers, no matter how skilled they were. Thus, the Scandinavian power never reached its peaks in France, at least not on the scale it did in England, Ireland, and Scotland. As the Viking Era went on, there were numerous raids, but none of them led to permanent victories. The greatest manifestation of Scandinavian influence in France remains a couple of small settlements established on the Seine River in the tenth century.

Eastern Europe was a different affair for the Vikings. There were raids, but nothing too violent, and no Scandinavian kingdom was established through armed forces. Nonetheless, Vikings made it into the heart of Russia, where they were subsequently "absorbed" into the native Slavonic population, calling themselves "the Rus" (Russians).

At the end of the 11th century, the raids began to stop and Viking leaders became a thing of the past. Norway, Sweden, and Denmark became united kingdoms. The first two were done with adventures, while the latter, Denmark, became somewhat of a force to be reckoned with and managed to amass its unruly, young, adventurous men into their royal military. The last historical Viking leader who adhered to the old tradition was Olaf II Haraldson, who lost his "title" in 1015 when he was crowned king of Norway.

The Other Side of Viking History

The writers and chronicles of the Viking Era had no qualms when it came to demonizing and denigrating the Scandinavian people who ravaged their land. Clerics, such as Alcuin of York, were especially dramatic in their account of Viking raids on monasteries and places of worship, describing the carnage in minute detail and painting the assailants as demonic beasts rather than people. No matter the artistic liberties that were taken by Anglo-Saxon clerics, we can't deny that Vikings carried out violent and destructive attacks. But reducing the Vikings only to their warrior ventures is a grave mistake.

These Scandinavian men were indeed great fighters and military tacticians, but they were also merchants, explorers, artists, storytellers, and poets. They came from a rich and complex culture that they shared and left behind in the numerous lands they conquered or settled in. The Vikings' maritime voyages seem to have always been driven by two factors. One is the raiding and the plundering, and the other the sheer sense of adventure and desire to discover new places. This led them to venture into the Faroes, around the eight century, which they used as a *longphort* (a fortified port) to advance across the Atlantic.

In 872, Viking colonists led by Ingolf Arnarson settled on Iceland, where they established a unique, independent society. This Icelandic settlement went on to become a republic, ruled by the Althing, an assembly of chieftains that is considered to be one of the earliest parliaments. From this Scandinavian settlement, we also have some of the earliest Viking-written history pieces, the *Islendingabok* - the history of Iceland and the *Landnamabok* - an account of the first Icelandic Viking settlers and the land lots they took as their own. Besides these historical pieces, the Vikings who colonized Iceland also kept a written account of the tumultuous relationship they had with Iceland's natives. In the *Islendingasogur* (The Icelandic Family Sagas), the Vikings speak of the feuds, betrayals, allegiances, and conflicts that marked their first 150 years of settling in Iceland. The tales from the *Islendingasogur* are today considered to be some of the most important pieces of European literature from the Middle Ages, and they show the Vikings' proficiency in composing prose of great power.

Iceland also served as a platform for further exploration. In 982, Eirik the Red, a chieftain with a fiery temperament was exiled from the Icelandic colony for his involvement in a murder case. Unphased by this development (perhaps due to his history of being an exile from Norway for another murder-related affair), Eirik decided to take to the sea, and he sailed west in search of a rumored land. A 300-kilometers voyage brought Eirik's longship to Greenland, a lush land that exceeded his wildest expectations. With this discovery on hand, Eirik the Red returned to Iceland, filled 25 longships with colonists, and established his own settlement in Greenland, one that would survive well into the 15th century.

Eirik's son, Leif, a name you are probably familiar with by now, outdid his father as an explorer, sailing further west and discovering Vinland, but as a colonist, he wasn't as prolific as Eirik. Leif tried to replicate his father's strategy, however, the hostility from the Native Americans was too much for the small number of Viking settlers to handle, and Vinland was subsequently abandoned.

Regardless of his success at colonizing America, Leif Eirikson has garnered the reputation of a great discoverer and explorer, and for a Viking, few things mattered more than one's reputation. Sure, attributes such as bravery and intelligence were sought after in a Viking warrior, but leaving a legacy behind and being remembered was the icing on the cake. An aphorism from the *Havamal*, a collection of Viking sayings, goes something like "*Everything dies, we, our cattle, our families, but one thing that never dies is a dead man's reputation.*" The language used in the

Havamal is a bit more sardonic, but I tried to give it a modern twist to better reflect the idea.

And this concludes our brief look into the Viking's history. Now you have a timeline for the Viking Age, and you have a better picture of who they were, where they came from, and the many places they settled in or conquered. Before we move on to take a more in-depth look at the Viking way of life and what it entailed, I thought it would be a great idea to say a few words about some famous Vikings who, just as Leif, managed to leave their mark on history and garner a reputation that would last throughout the ages.

Famous Vikings and Heroes

Ivar the Boneless is part legend and part historical character. You might remember that he and his brother Haldfan were the leaders of the great army that took Northumbria and Eastern Anglia by storm. Ivar also led attacks in Ireland

and he is considered a founding father of the Viking rule in the kingdom of Dublin. Not much is recorded about him after the year 870, but it is presumed that he led attacks and ruled in the Islands of Man, Ireland, and other places around the Irish seas.

In Viking sagas, Ivar is the son of Ragnar Lothbroke, and his attack on Northumbria is an act of revenge against its king for killing his father. As for his peculiar nickname, its clear origin is unknown. Some historians believe that it stems from his fighting style and flexibility, which gave the illusion of him being "boneless," while others think it's a sly remark regarding his masculinity (alluding to him being impotent). An Irish annal notes the year 873 as the date of his death.

Sigurd is a legendary Norse hero who appears in many stories. Although different sources propose variations regarding his character and fate, he is usually portrayed as being strong, courageous, and successful in his endeavors. In earlier accounts, Sigurd is described as being of noble lineage, which might hint at a potential historical origin and his connection with an old Scandinavian ruler. In the *Prose Edda,* we find one of Sigurd's most famous legends - the slaying of the great dragon Fafnir. The saga speaks of how Sigur stabbed the beast and tasted its blood, gaining the ability to understand the language of the birds. This allows him to find out Reginn's plan to murder him to acquire the dragon's treasure. Thus, Sigurd kills Reginn and keeps the gold for himself. He then marries the daughter of a king and helps his brother-in-law, Gunnar, ask for the valkyrie Bruhild's hand in marriage. But in doing so, he tricks the valkyrie by taking Gunnar's form to complete Brunhild's challenges. This whole plot ends up leading to Sigurd's demise when Brunhild takes her revenge for being tricked. In a different version, Gunnar kills Sigurd when he believes that the hero had slept with Brunhild.

In many stories of Sigurd's life, Brunhild is the one that inevitably gets him killed, in one way or another. But other legends see the courageous hero becoming a king of the Franks or learning the magic of the runes from the valkyrie Sigrdrifa (which is another one of Brunhild's names). Due to all the variations, we can say that Sigurd's tale is open-ended, leaving space for interpretations and choosing which version better suits our preferences.

Eirik Bloodaxe is often portrayed as the stereotypical Viking fighter, with an overly Viking nickname. His accomplishments include being the king of Northumbria as well as the king of Norway. However, this last honor came to him in a rather dishonorable way. To become first in the line of succession he and his wife, Gunnhild, killed five of his brothers, earning Eirik his nickname "Bloodaxe" as well as the ire of his people. When Hakon the Good, another brother of his, rose to fight him for the throne, Eirik received no support whatsoever from the Norway people, and he chose to flee for his life. Not a very Viking-like action for him. Rumors at the time praised Eirik for his abilities as a fighter but condemned him for being dominated and too easily influenced by Gunnhild. So, despite his accomplishments, Eirik is not very close to the classical Viking hero.

Cnut the Great definitely beats Eirik when it comes to his Viking reputation. He was the son of a Danish king, Svein Forkbeard, who had managed to conquer England in 1013. But Svein's luck was tough, and he died shortly after asserting his claim over the lands. His oldest son, Harald, inherited the Danish throne, and poor Cnut received the mission to reinstate Viking control over England, which was already back in Anglo-Saxon hands. The young man rose to the challenge, and in 1016, he conquered England and married the last king's widow to cement his position. In the years to follow, Cnut also became king of Denmark (apparently through peaceful means) and the king of Norway (which he conquered in 1028). Thus, Cnut became the ruler of the largest North Sea empire of the Middle Ages.

Although Cnut would use the good old' Viking tactic of warfare to keep England in check, he was arguably a good ruler. Under him, the towns became important administrative and economic centers. Denmark flourished with material wealth and an influx of innovative ideas. Cnut also developed a coinage system, firmly established the Christian Church, and is known for going to Rome on a peaceful pilgrimage to meet the Pope in person. From this point of view, Cnut can be seen as closer to an Anglo-Saxon king than a Viking ruler and conqueror. Ironically, Cnut's ability to adapt to different circumstances and cultures makes him, to some degree, the ultimate Viking, for this flexibility allowed the Scandinavians to be so successful in their European endeavors.

Helgi Hundingsbane is another legendary Norse hero that may or may not be based on a real historical figure. It is said that on the night of his birth, the Norns had foreseen a great future for Helgi, decreeing that he will become one of the greatest princes that will ever exist. This is perhaps why his parents Sigmundr and Borghildr had named him Helgi, after another famous epic hero, Helgi Hjotvarosson. It is also theorized that our Helgi was the reincarnation of the late eponymous hero because their fates ended up being strikingly similar. Back to our story; when he was a youngster, Helgi disguised himself to explore the court of king Hunding, an enemy of his father's. He almost got caught, but he managed to escape, and Helgi later killed Hunding, earning him the name "Hundingsbane." Then the Valkyrie Sigrun called for his aid to help her escape an unwanted marriage.

Helgi fought for Sigrun and came up victorious, even though Sigrun's father and brother were slain. He then married her, and the pair had many children. All was fine and well until Dagr, another brother of Sigrun, had called for Odin's aide to avenge his fallen brethren. Odin listened to his plea and offered him his mighty spear, with which Dagr killed Helgi. However, Odin had picked him to be part of his honorable warriors in Valhalla. Helgi and Sigrun had one last final meeting before his departure for the realm of the honorable dead. It is said that Sigrun's sorrow was so deep that she too perished, not long after her beloved.

Aud the Deep-minded and **Freydis Eiriksdottir** are two famous Viking women with very different stories but a similar fiery spirit. For the most part of her life, Aud was the poster wife and mother. She married the king of Dublin, Olaf the White, in the mid-ninth century and gave birth to their only son, Thorstein the Red. After Olaf's death, she and Thorstein moved to Scotland, where he established himself as a great warrior. Thorstein ruled over most of Scotland before dying a Viking's death in battle. Aud understood that she could not recover her importance in Scotland without her son, so she took her grandchildren and fled for the new Iceland colony, which seemed very promising. Aud took her family, friends, and a couple of Irish and Scottish slaves (who she later freed to garner their loyalty). She chose a large piece of Icelandic land for her and her entourage. She is considered to be one of the great founding colonists of Iceland, and many great medieval Icelandic families could trace their ancestry back to Aud the Deep-minded. She was definitely a strong, Viking woman who knew how to take the opportunities that life gave her and make the most out of them.

Freydis's fate was strikingly different. She was the daughter of Eirik the Red and, consequently, Leif's sister. Freydis was deeply involved in her brother's attempts to colonize Vinland. She was part of the group that initiated contact with the Native American population. At first, their relationships were friendly, but soon the natives turned on her men. Freydis was a true Viking warrior and, despite being in the later terms of her pregnancy, she picked up a sword and was ready to smite her attackers. Thankfully, at the sight of a murderous pregnant woman, the natives ran for the hills to save their lives.

On a different account, we see Freydis's bad side. During another attempt to conquer Vinland, she discovered that the group she traveled with had brought more people aboard her ship than she had agreed to. Furious, she pushed her husband and his men to slaughter all the unwelcome crewmates. And so they did, except for the women, who they did not want to kill. Then Freydis took the gnarly task upon herself and killed the understandably frightened women. She also forced her men to take an oath that what happened on the ship would never transpire on their return to the Greenland colony. Not much else is known about Freydis, the daughter of Eirik the Red, but from what we know, we can guess that she either died in battle or went on to die a more peaceful death.

Einar Buttered-Bread is well-known for a tale of treachery from the *Orkneyinga saga* in which he played a simple pawn rather than the leading role. I wanted to end the list of the famous Vikings with him because Einar has a rather unique story. He was the grandson of the Earl of Orkney, Thorfinn Skullsplitter, and he was tricked by Ragnhild, Eirik Bloodaxe's daughter, to take part in the fight over the Orkney earldom. Ragnhild was a smart, driven woman who knew how to manipulate others into her schemes. She was first married to Thorfinn's heir, Arnfinn, but she had him killed, and she made his brother Harvard Harvest-Happy earl in his stead. She went on to marry Harvard, after which she immediately started to conspire with Einar, to get him removed. Ragnhild promised Einar to make him earl of Orkney if he killed Harvard, who, let's not forget, was Einar's uncle.

Einar Buttered-Bread completed his part of the deal, but Ragnhild had other plans. While her second husband was getting murdered at her orders, she instigated Einar's cousin, Einar Hard-mouth to kill him and become the earl. But the web of treachery goes even deeper! Hard-mouth himself was then killed by Ljot, yet another cousin, who went on to claim both the earldom and Ragnhild as his. Was this Ragnhild's plan all along? We have no way of knowing, but I like to think of it that way.

As for poor Einar, that's where his story ended. The only mystery that remains is that of his peculiar name. After all, Butter-Bread is not really a tough Viking warrior name that inspires fear and awe. But this mystery, just like Ragnhild's plot, is to remain unsolved.

Chapter 2: The Viking Life

We've seen the power and force of this warrior civilization. Still, the Viking way of life can't be reduced to naval endeavors and great battles. In fact, a closer look at the Vikings' daily lives shows a far more ordinary picture than we'd like to imagine.

Typical Settlements and Agriculture

Most Vikings lived in rural areas, where their main focus was agriculture. The settlements themselves were relatively small, and they consisted of somewhere around fifteen to fifty farms per village. Trade towns existed, but they were so far and few between that only an incredibly small percent of the population lived there. Additionally, isolated farms built-in remote areas such as mountains, forests, or fjords were pretty common, and so were villages that comprised only two or three farmsteads. Cemeteries were placed right at the edges of villages or farmsteads, serving as a morbid representation of one's claim over the land (because their ancestors had lived, worked, and died there). Not very poetic but rather successful at showing your legitimacy of owning the said plot of land.

Men would occupy themselves with taking care of the land, involving themselves in fertilizing the soil, sowing, and plowing while women took upon themselves tasks that were performed mainly inside the house, such as cooking and producing clothing and alcoholic drinks. Harvesting the crops usually fell on the entire family since it was a laborious task that required all hands on deck. The care for farm animals was also divided between men and women. During the summer the men would take the cattle and the sheep out to graze and watch over them, and during the winter, when the animals were kept inside to protect them from the cold, the women would cater to them, milking them and keeping their enclosures clean. Speaking of farm animals, horses were cherished by Vikings. They represented the main form of transportation of both men and their goods, even in the coldest parts of Scandinavia where the snowfall was substantial. In such areas, horses would pull sleds and be fitted with spiked footwear to allow them to cross frozen lands and bodies of water.

Back to farming, Vikings plowed their lands using an almost-vertical, wooden scratch plow that was pulled by oxen or slaves. The wooden spike did the job of breaking up the soil, but it didn't turn it. That is why Viking fields were cross-plowed, by plowing a second row of lines intersecting with the first. Because the plow was wooden, it would often break after a few days of wear, and it would have to be replaced - iron plows came after the end of the Viking Age. The Norsemen practiced crop rotation, alternating which fields were sown to allow them to rejuvenate naturally, and they used animal and human waste as fertilizer. To harvest, men used scythes to cut the crops and women had rakes to expose the grains. Then men would prepare the grains with precise club-strikes, and hand mills were used to ground them. Once the process was done and over, women could use the resulting material for baking, cooking, and making beer or other alcoholic beverages.

Ironworking was practiced on farmsteads, and it was reserved to fulfill the needs of the household. Professional smiths would practice their craft in the few urban areas, and they would often trade their goods in exchange for food. Most physically demanding tasks were carried out by the slaves that the Vikings captured during the raids or in battles for supremacy. Although one can look at this farming-centric life through rose-colored glasses, it was far from an idyllic situation. Sure, Vikings had slaves to carry out the unpleasant tasks or do hard work, but taking care of the land still required incredible effort and labor to accomplish even the easiest tasks. Besides that, these Viking farmers lived in constant fear of famine, natural disasters, or raids that would deprive them of their crops and, consequently, their means of living. Diseases were rampant at the time, and famine loomed over the lands. It wasn't uncommon for children to die before reaching adulthood, and the image of the strong, muscular Viking warrior may not be as close to the truth as we think it is.

With their at-home situation looking so grim, it's not hard to understand why raiding and establishing settlements on other lands became such a big focus for Vikings. They just wanted a better life for themselves and their families. And they were willing to do anything to accomplish that.

Social Classes

The Vikings had three main social classes: the slaves, the free men, and the earls. Their social hierarchy was similar in nature to that of other European civilizations of that time.

The slaves were the lowest class of the Viking society. There were three ways in which one could become a slave. One was, as I already mentioned, being captured in a war or raid. Vikings believed that the ones who they had spared in battle needed to pay them back with their freedom for being allowed to live. From the Vikings' point of view, this was a fair trade, and that's how they justified slavery. The second way to become a slave was to be born to a slave. The descendants of slaves were also slaves, a logic justified by the same "your freedom for the gift of life" principle. Lastly, one could become a slave if they went bankrupt. A poor person could give up their freedom to someone who was of higher status in exchange for gathering that person's protection. More often than not, that was the only choice these poor people had, especially when debts were involved. They simply had nothing else to give but their freedom, so they would willingly become someone's slave to have their material needs (such as food, clothes, and shelter) taken care of. It was a steep price to pay, but it was a better alternative to dying of hunger or at the hands of creditors.

Slaves were mainly used for farm work, but it wasn't uncommon for masters to sell their slaves into the slave trade business that was already flourishing in Europe. There are also a few accounts of slaves being sacrificed after their master's death, following the beliefs that they had to continue to fulfill their roles in the afterlife. From being subjected to inhumane amounts of labor to being sold into the slave trade network or being sacrificed during their master's funerary rites, it's more than fair to say that Viking slaves had few prospects.

Mostly, the Viking society consisted of free men. These were farmers (the wealthier ones had their own land, and the less fortunate worked the other's lands in exchange for permission to harvest a plot for themselves), merchants, craftsmen, and warriors. The majority of Vikings who took part in raids and great battles were free men. In the Viking society, the older a son was, the more he would inherit from his father, so the younger children would often be left with scraps. That's why Viking warriors were mainly young men, with nothing tying them down to a place, looking to make a name and material situation for themselves. They sought silver and plots of land for farming in the areas that would become colonies and settlements. These young men simply wanted something better than the little they had at home and, because they enjoyed the protection of the law and had the means to improve their financial situation, there was nothing that could stop them from doing so.

The *jarls* (earls) were at the top of the Viking social hierarchy. They were mostly chieftains who became wealthy through plundering and raiding. In the later years of the Viking Age, earls were closer to what we call aristocrats, serving as the king's subordinates and appropriating as much land as they pleased.

Viking Politics

Throughout most of the Viking period, the political power was in the hands of clan leaders and chieftains, who exerted their control over small groups of people. They led bands in raids and vicious attacks while also competing with other fellow chieftains for power and dominance. To assert their position, chieftains needed to find great and loyal warriors that would stand by his side and bring him great success. And earning the loyalty of Vikings was no easy deed. A chieftain had to be fearless, generous with his man, always victorious in battles, and he had to have a good reputation. Success in battle was pretty much the means to everything, and the wealth they gained allowed them to be generous and "inspire" poets and storytellers to build up their reputation. These stories and epic sagas would then reach young men who wanted to fight under such a famous chieftain, growing the numbers of the warlord's armies and thus helping him be more successful in battle. It was an efficient cycle that smart chieftains knew how to work in their favor.

Wealth during the early Viking period was not expressed through coins. Warlords dispensed silver, gold, and arm rings, which ranged from simple to exquisitely ornate. Plots of lands were also commonly used as a trading coin since having land was a fundamental element of Viking success. Chieftains would reward their men by throwing great feasts, that were usually intertwined with religious elements. The generosity of the chieftains came at a simple but essential price: loyalty. This attribute was very important in Viking society. One of the greatest honors for a warrior was to die in battle alongside their chieftain, proving that their loyalty is not only tied to economic gain. Sure, wealth was an incentive, but Viking warriors wanted more. They sought honor and a sense of belongingness, which a great leader could artfully provide.

Besides these warlords who held control over particular regions, the power was held by a legal assembly. This institution ruled through laws, and it was highly respected. Legal assemblies were held in outdoor areas, and during these gatherings, free men would recite, amend, or make new laws. Slaves didn't have the right to participate, and women could only contribute when serving as representatives for male relatives. By modern standards, these Viking assemblies had legislative and judicial functions, but on a smaller scale. It was perfectly possible for two Nordic villages to have different sets of rules because the assemblies were local and had only local power. Since the assemblies had no executive branch, the decisions were enforced by the victorious party (for disputes) or by the community. If, for example, someone was fined and they refused or failed to pay, they would become outlaws. As an outlaw, you were no longer under the protection of the law, so anyone could kill you. Because this system was efficient enough, the assembly did not need an executive branch to carry out their dirty work. The Icelandic Althing was a more developed form of legal assembly with deep roots in politics, making it more similar to the form of government we have in the present days.

Speaking of politics, as chieftains became more and more influential, the battle for supremacy intensified. The most successful leaders in battle amassed greater armies of good, loyal warriors, and soon enough some armies grew large enough to conquer others. The most powerful leaders declared themselves kings over wide areas, to the terror of Medieval Europe that would now face greater, more organized attacks. The transition from warlords to kings didn't happen at once in the Scandinavian region. Denmark came first, followed by Norway, and Sweden, where the process went beyond the historical Viking Age. The switch from chieftains to kings was more than a power shift; it was also a shift in role and tradition. Viking kings, such as Cnut the Great, had more in common with European rulers than traditional warlords. The great scale of power made it impossible for kings to maintain that close, loyalty-based relationship with their men. Things were now more structured and bureaucratic. There were also rules in place regarding governance and succession and taxes were introduced. Interestingly, this shift in politics happened at the same time as the one in religion, with the Norsemen converting to Christianity (more on this in a later chapter!), so we can wholeheartedly say that this was an era of change for the Vikings.

With the introduction of Christianity, the relationship between the people and their king was formulated in religious terms. They were to serve their king unconditionally, just as they did God, swerving even further from the traditional Viking chieftain-warrior relationship. Although the rise of kings made Vikings a more organized and successful military force, it also represented the "death" of the old Viking way of life, leading to the end of the great Viking Age.

Commerce

The Norse people had one of the greatest trade networks of the Middle Ages, stretching as far as Baghdad and Asia. This feat is even more extraordinary if we look back at the simple way of life of early eight century Vikings. They were farmers who rarely produced more than their household needed to survive, and few people lived in urban areas where trade was common. But these "trade towns," regardless of how small they were, propelled the Scandinavian people into the vast Eurasian trade networks, starting a new age of commerce. With trade towns on the rise, people began to specialize in crafts, understanding the huge opportunity that foreign trade represented. Jewelers, blacksmiths, antler workers, and many more migrated to the trade towns where they would produce their goods mainly for export.

The most cherished Scandinavian trade items were by far furs. The cold Nordic climate was home to animals with thick, warm pelts that were coveted and prized abroad. Another pillar of the Viking trade was slaves, as it was for many civilizations in Eurasia at the time. The Viking slaves were, let's not forget, people that were captured in raids. And since it was not uncommon for Vikings to raid other Viking settlements, many of the slaves that were traded were Norsemen themselves. To the Vikings, it didn't matter much whether you were a foreigner or a Scandinavian, a Christian, or a worshipper of the Norse gods. All that mattered was your market value. The Vikings were very pragmatic in that way. Additionally, since trade towns were flourishing at the time, the abundance of valuable trade goods made them alluring targets for potential raids. Commerce was a brutal affair in the Viking age, even between Norsemen themselves.

For Viking chieftains of that time, trade was simply a way to garner more wealth and luxury goods. These gave them status and allowed them to be very generous with their men, strengthening loyalties and their power as leaders. For the Viking farmers, the rise of the trade towns gave them an opportunity to buy commodities in exchange for food or whatever goods they produced on their farmstead. Around the year 1000, due to the changes in politics and the switch to kings, the luxurious trade towns almost vanished, leaving space for market places that mainly focused on commodities and that were more accessible to the regular people. This is yet another way in which the shift to a more European type of society had negative repercussions for the Viking civilization.

Gender Roles in the Viking Age

We've gone through quite a few aspects of Viking life, and I've presented two outstanding Viking women, Aud the Deep-minded and Freydis Eiriksdottir, who held important positions in the Scandinavian society. But did the Vikings have an equal society? Were the Viking shield-maidens a reality or a figment of our feminist desires?

Well, the Viking society, just as many others of the time, gave men a higher social status than women, and they judged someone's worth based on how well they fulfilled their designated role. Men had to be manly, great warriors and/or farmers, and women had to ace housekeeping duties. The societal role of women was traditional in the sense that they were expected to be wives and mothers. On the bright side, a woman who could fulfill her role was greatly appreciated by her family and Viking society. But their appreciation never quite reached the level of the respect and reputation that men could garner. Great women had no stories made about them, no poems to speak about their deeds, and no songs to sing their accomplishments. But at least they got some recognition, which is more than many women in the Middle Ages could hope for.

Viking women didn't have much of a say when it came to marriage; the proposal came from a man, and the bride-to-be's family negotiated terms on her behalf and decided if the proposal was to be accepted or refused. Yes, the poor woman had no say in this. Adultery was also a capital sin for women, as their husbands were allowed by law to kill both their cheating wife and her suitor if they caught them in the act. Some Viking settlements had laws for men caught committing adultery, but the punishments were more lenient, as it was somewhat more socially acceptable for a man to cheat than a woman. It was commonplace for warlords and kings alike to have multiple wives and maybe some concubines on the side, but the women were expected to be loyal to their husbands. A pretty standard idea for the Middle Ages.

Women did, however, have the right to divorce their husbands. Women who found themselves in unhappy, abusive, or otherwise bad marriages, and who could prove their husbands' wrongdoings, were allowed to divorce them and would receive monetary compensation, to ensure that they could provide for themselves. When it came to careers though, women couldn't aspire to anything else except for being housewives. Only men could work the land, hold political power, speak in assemblies, become warriors, and leave their homeland. Sure there are stories of women going into battle alongside their men, and some artifacts showing that women were skilled in warfare and owned weapons, but as of now, we don't have enough scientific evidence to say this was the norm. They could have been exceptions to the norm. As of the mythical valkyries - the winged female warriors who took men to Valhalla, their historical counterparts were most likely sorceresses and not female fighters. The sorceresses were women who, allegedly, could use magic to aid Vikings in battle. But their magic could only influence the outcome of the wars, so their presence on the battlefield was not necessary.

Since we brought magic to the mix, that is one thing that belonged only to women. It was socially acceptable for women to practice *seidr* (Norse magic), but men that delved into such practices were deeply despised and sometimes even killed for their affinities. For some reason, Vikings saw magic as something akin to homosexuality, which brought dishonor for the overly masculine Norse warriors. And since women were seen as weak and, obviously feminine, they were free to flaunt their magic powers in bright daylight without anyone giving them the stink-eye. So, that's one point for the women, I guess?

These would be the generalities on gender roles, but as with any rules, there were exceptions. High-status women did exist in the Viking Age. Most of them had garnered this status through marriage or being born in an aristocratic family, but they had status nonetheless. Women could also inherit properties, if there were no male heirs, and indulge in artistic endeavors such as poetry - although there are few accounts of female poets. While Viking women did not have it good, they definitely had more liberties and overall better quality of life than their contemporaries in other nations, who were treated pretty much as a man's property and were considered disposable.

Food, Clothing, Jewelry, and Weapons of the Viking Age

Although not as captivating as other subjects, I think it's good to have at least some idea of these aspects of a Viking's life.

Starting with the food, different parts of the Scandinavian region offered different resources. Speaking on general terms, the most cultivated grain in the Viking world was barley, which was used for bread loaves and bread buns. Other plants and grains that would be added to the traditional bread recipe include oats, flax, rye, and pine bark. A Viking's diet also included plentiful dairy products, because they had sheep, goats, and cattle. The proximity to the sea made fish a common element of Viking foods, with the favorites being herring and cod. And of course, we can't forget about meat - the Scandinavians had many options when it came to this dietary element. The meat came from farm animals such as pigs, cows, and chicken, as well as from hunting. The Vikings hunted a wide array of beasts from deer, rabbits, and wild boars to seals and whales. The latter two were considered delicacies and their oils were used for cooking or as butter substitutes.

Because they were strong warriors, they did not skip on fruits and veggies. Vikings cultivated cabbage, peas, beets, and beans, and they gathered from the wild blackberries, strawberries, pears, cherries, hazelnuts, and others. Another interesting aspect of Viking meals is that they loved spices and aromatic herbs. Their meals often included parsley, garlic, thyme, mustard, cumin, salt (extracted by boiling salt water), and honey (as a sweetener). The staple Viking beverages were mead and beer, made from honey and barley. These alcoholic beverages would usually be drunk from cattle horns or wooden cups (if they wanted to enjoy their drink). Vikings also made fruit wines, but because they didn't know how to distill alcohol these were pretty tame. Luxury wines brought from abroad would usually be served in silver bowls or imported glass vessels, for a touch of refinement.

Viking clothing was mainly made from wool and flax (from which comes linen), to provide warmth, and was worn in layers to protect them from the harsh climate. Women produced the clothing by spinning the materials and weaving them into garments. It was a long and arduous process, which is why richer families would buy commercially-made fabrics. Linen was preferred for undergarments because it felt nicer on the skin, and fur was typically used for cloaks and decorative trimmings. Natural dyes were used to spice up the simple, white clothing (because the Scandinavian sheep were predominantly white) but they were of low quality and they faded quickly. Calfskin and goatskin were used for boots. Linen or silk bands were used as hair ties for both men and women.

The clothing itself was pretty typical, with shirts, breeches, and tunics for men and linen chemises and woolen dresses for women. Silks, adornments, and fancy embroideries were reserved for the wealthy. As a side note here, the popular portrayal of Vikings as being unkempt is far from the truth. They valued their physical appearance and they used utensils such as razors, combs, and tweezers to take care of themselves. They also didn't live in huts, but in halls that were maintained by the women and would house feasts whenever there was a reason for celebrating.

Jewelry for the Vikings served two purposes: to show one's status and to act as forms of payment if the need arose. They consisted of rings, necklaces, brooches, pendants, and amulets. The most popular amulets of the time were representations of Thor's hammer, miniature thrones (which were linked with the worship of Odin), and crosses (when Vikings switched to Christianity).

In the Viking Era, all free men had the duty to own weapons. Swords were the staple weapons of the Norse society, and only the elite had the honor of carrying one. Many poets and song-writers would mention the swords of warlords in their works, using artistic metaphors such as "flame of Odin." At the start of the eighth century, most swords were single-edged, but as the Viking age went on, iron double-edged swords became more popular. Axes were the weapons of choice for the common people. They served both as tools and weapons, and they were simply made. All that distinguished one ax from another was the shape and size, which varied a lot. Viking spears were either for throwing or thrusting, and they were a staggering half a meter long. Bows and arrows were used for both hunting and war, although those taken to the battle were rudimentary and simply put together.

Viking shields were made from wood and they were heavily decorated with mythical motifs of colorful symbols. Chainmail was reserved for the wealthy, but helmets were worn by the great majority of Vikings. They were made from leather or iron and were rounded, with simple designs. So no, they didn't wear horned helmets, mostly because they were impractical in combat. The more you know.

The Old Norse

The Vikings spoke the Old Norse language, and all the texts that we have from the Viking Age are written using it. Old Norse evolved from a northern dialect of the Proto-germanic language, and it is part of the Germanic family of languages like modern German and English. By the beginning of the Viking Age, around the year 750, the dialect had transformed into Proto-Norse, becoming a new language altogether. Even so, because the Vikings were spread all around Europe and in many other regions, the Old Norse had many regional dialects that were still pretty close to each other. The Old Norwegian and the Old Icelandic were about as different as North American English is to British English. Something to note here would be that, because most of the texts that survived from the Viking Era come from Iceland, what we presently refer to as Old Norse is actually the Iceland dialect of Old Norse.

From a grammatical point of view, the Old Norse had a free word order, with few rules regarding positioning, such as an object had to follow a verb. Only pronouns had separate dual forms, and verbs were inflected for mood, number, tense, and person. The first syllable of a word was always stressed, and the following could be either short or long. For written texts, the Vikings used the Younger Futhark alphabet, a runic script that was later replaced by the Latin alphabet when most of Scandinavia converted to Christianity.

Old Norse is considered to be the parent language of modern Icelandic, Norwegian and Faroese.

Valhalla and Viking Individualism

Valhalla or the Hall of Slain Warriors was pretty much the Viking interpretation of Heaven. If a Viking died an honorable death, in battle, he would be taken by a Valkyrie into Valhalla, where Odin himself would welcome them. Depiction of Valhalla in Norse literature describes it as an incredible hall, with golden shields adorning the roof and rafters made of spears. There, the warriors would fight all day to keep their skills sharp and feast all night to celebrate their great deeds. Feasting and fighting do sound like a Viking's greatest pleasures, right? These honored dead men, known as *einherjar* would spend their afterlife preparing for *Ragnarok* (the end of the world) and feasting from the meat of Saehrimnir, a boar that came back to life every night to satisfy the men's hunger and drinking Heidrun's mead (a goat that produced the finest alcoholic beverage).

However, out of the warriors who died in battle, only half made it to Valhalla. The ones that were not chosen by the mighty Valkyries would go to the field of Freya, where they would spend their afterlife offering their company to women who died as maidens. Some would argue that this sort of afterlife is more appealing than being stuck in a perpetual cycle of fighting and feasting, but again these are Vikings and to them, Valhalla was the ultimate goal. The Vikings who died of sickness or old age would go to Hel (the Underworld, also referred to as *Niflheim*). This place is not equivalent to our concept of Hell, but rather a less satisfying version of Valhalla. The dead were being taken care of by Hel, the goddess of the underworld. But there was a special place in Niflheim for adulterers, murderers, and other evil-doers, where they would pay for their bad deeds and where a dragon ate their corpses, an imaginative punishment.

Now, something that I felt I should touch on before we dive into the Norse mythology is the character of the Vikings. We tend to see them as a somewhat patriotic civilization who put loyalty above personal gain and interests. But the Vikings were pretty selfish. They put themselves first, even if that meant betraying their own kin, just as we've seen in the case of Vikings enslaving other Norsemen to sell them on the slave market. The Norse idea of self only existed in relation to one's actions and social standing. The way you acted and the relationships you had made you who you were, so Vikings were somewhat constricted to be loyal to family, friends, and their leaders to not risk being considered unhonorable. Even so, the Viking society was permissive and it allowed people to choose their social relationships. That gave Vikings the liberty to refuse or accept obligations, for the most part. Their society was not as lenient on women, and certain obligations such as those for family and one's chieftain could not be refused.

The men who achieved greatness would be celebrated by name, in songs and poems, making them immortal in a sense. The graves of Vikings were individual, and they were decorated according to the person's life and achievements, another measure to ensure that someone's valiant deeds would not be forgotten. Remember, reputation was everything to the Norse people. The selfish individualism of Vikings is also apparent in their relationships with the higher beings, the gods. The Scandinavians worshipped them, and "served" them in the same way that they served their warlords, to garner favors and riches.

These are the Vikings; they treasured the ideals of honor and loyalty but what they ultimately desired was personal glory and immortality through great reputation. From this point onward in the book, we'll go into the mythical world of the Vikings and we'll discover the Norse gods and how the Northmen worshipped them. It's finally time to drink from that Well of Knowledge and meet Odin and his entourage of gods and goddesses.

Chapter 3: The Norse Myth of Creation

One thing I learned in all my years of studying mythology is that the best way to get into a new mythological realm is to start with the beginning, and that is the myth of creation. All cultures and religions have their version of how the world came to be and the Vikings make no exception. In fact, this book had actually started with the first few lines of the Norse creation myth, to give you a little taste of what was to come later and get you into the mystic atmosphere of the Viking mythos. How about we pick up from where I left it in the Introduction, and then we'll establish some basic notions about Nordic mythology.

The Birth of the Giants and the Aesir Gods

Ymir (the Screamer), the first living creature,

born in Ginnungagap from the melted ice of Niflheim, was a giant and a force of destruction. He was also a hermaphrodite who could reproduce on his own. As he slept, the giant started to sweat, and from the sweat of his armpits, a man and a woman were born, while from the sweat of his legs emerged another man. This is how the first frost giants were born into this world. From the ice that was still melting in the void, another creature was brought into being - the cow Audhumla. She would lick salty ice blocks for nourishment and she graciously offered her rivers of milk for Ymir to feast on and grow.

While liking the salt, Audhumla found and uncovered a man - Buri (the Progenitor), the first of the Aesir gods. Buri was a strong handsome man, and he had a son called Bor. He then married Besla, the daughter of a frost giant. This unlikely pair of god and giant had three children: Odin, Vili, and Ve.

The Creation of the World and the First Men

One day, Odin and his brothers killed Ymir. The amount of blood that poured from Ymir's wound was so tremendous that it flooded Ginnungagap, drowning almost all the frost giants. Only Belgemir and his wife managed to escape, and he fathered the giants that came after. Odin, Vili, and Ve carried Ymir's corpse to the middle of the void and they built the world from his carcass. They made seas, oceans, and lakes from Ymir's blood, they used his muscles and his skin to brandish the Earth, from his hair they made trees and vegetation, they constructed mountains from his bones (except for the skull, that comes a bit later) and from his teeth, they made pebbles and rocks. A bit hard to imagine but bear with me. The gods then turned the creatures that fed on Ymir's body into dwarves. They would become great craftsmen that could create anything, from jewelry to magical weapons, such as the legendary hammer Mjolnir.

The gods used Ymir's skull to create the sky, and they placed a dwarf at each corner (north, south, east, and west), to keep the skull floating above the Earth. For clouds, they used Ymir's brains, and for stars, they gathered flying embers from Muspelheim. The newly created Earth was surrounded by waters, and the sons of Bor gave the land that was close to the sea to the giants, to settle and live there. But since the giants were hostile beings, the gods wanted a place to protect them from the creatures' fury, so from Ymir's eyebrows (or eyelashes in some versions), they created a stronghold inland, far from the sea. They called this citadel Midgard. A side note here, this great sea was also the abode of *Jurmurgandr*, the giant serpent who is said to have been so enormous that it could coil itself around the entire world. Yet another reason to keep humans away from the waters.

While walking around the shores, Odin and his brothers found two trees from which they decided to create a man and a woman, the first humans.

Odin gave them the spark of life, Vili gave them consciousness, and Ve gifted them with clothes and identities. The first man received the name Ask, and the first woman Embla. The sons of Bor built a fence around Midgard and gave the stronghold to the humans, to keep them safe while they grew in numbers.

One human, called Mundilfari, had two children who were so radiant that he named them Sol (Sun) and Mani (Moon). When the gods found out about Mundilfari's arrogance (yes they saw him being proud and giving fancy names to his children as arrogance) they punished him by taking Sol and Mani and putting them in the sky, to light it up during the day and respectively night. They both rode chariots and were pursued by two wolves, Hati (Hate) and Skoll (Treachery). At Ragnarok, the end of the world, it is said that the wolves would catch and eat the sun and moon. In a different version of this myth, Mundilfari is replaced with the giant Norvi, who had only a daughter called Nott (Night). She had a son named Dagr (Day), and the pair would ride chariots across the sky to bring day and night. The two wolves Hati and Skoll are present in this version of the myth, still chasing the chariots in hopes of devouring the sun and the moon.

Asgard and the Aesir

Odin and his brothers now wanted to build a place for their own kind, so they went to the middle of the world and created Asgard. Many stories in the Norse mythology happen in Asgard, and there lived almost all the important gods we'll later discuss. Asgard had a great hall called Hlidskjalf, where Odin sat on a high chair, kind of like a throne, from which he could see the whole world and understand everything that was going on.

Odin went on to marry Frigg, and their descendants, known as Aesir, would inhabit Asgards and its kingdoms. Because he created men and fathered the Aesir gods Odin is also known as the "All-Father." His first child was the mighty and powerful Thor, who dominated every living creature with his strength. Other remarkable Aesir gods are Loki, Baldr, Tyr, and Heimdall. The main sanctuary of the Aesir is the tree of life, Yggdrasil, where they hold their court and their feasts. Yggdrasil is said to have been the greatest tree that ever existed, with branches that reached the heavens and spread out over the world. Its roots reach all the other realism, including that of men and that of giants, *Jutunheim*. Nidhogg, a dragon of death, feeds from the roots of Yggdrasil while the Norns (the three fates) decide the fates of the humans at the base of the great tree.

The Aesir and the Vanir

Odin might be the father of the Aesir gods, but not all Norse deities are part of this family. There is a second, smaller family called the Vanir, which contains fertility deities, gods of climate, and deities of harvest. For obvious reasons, the Vanir gods such as Freyja, Freyr, and Njord were very popular in farming communities, while the Aesir, who were usually connected with government and war, were mainly worshipped by kings and warriors. In Norse mythology, the two families are portrayed as being in a constant state of conflict, to the point of there being numerous Aesir-Vanir wars.

However, these wars always end with peace and with the deities fusing their families together. This peace reflects the Viking concept that society needs both social classes, the farmers and the warriors, to function and prosper.

Analyzing the Myth of Creation

As fascinating as it is, the Norse myth of creation is, unceremoniously said, weird and it requires a closer examination of its themes if we want to understand the concepts that lay hidden at its core. One of the first things we are introduced to in this story is the abyss Ginnungagap and the frost giant Ymir. These are both personifications of the idea of the chaos that comes before creation and its limitless potential. They are "nothingness" in the sense that they don't represent something material, but they contain what the gods need in order to create everything they want or need. After all, Ymir, a crude personification of chaos, is the creator of the first beings, and the sons of Bor use his body to build the world as the Norse saw it.

In Viking mythology, the frost giants are always characterized as beings who want to corrupt the world and destroy the order created by the Aesir gods. They are chaotic in nature, just like Ymir was, and they instinctively seek destructions. But, they also present the potential to create great things. The giants are described as having great abilities such as that to brew ale, craft enormous cauldrons, create runes and meads with magical properties, and so on. In many stories and legends, the gods recognize the resources that giants possess and they attempt to steal them for personal use or to benefit the Norse culture. In a way, we can say that the Aesir gods see giants as nothing more but raw materials, that they can mold and shape to their own advantage. Ymir is simply the first mythological account of this concept of gods using the chaotic potential of giants.

Another interesting thing about Ymir is that he is characterized as being a hermaphrodite, that can reproduce on his own. That is mostly because the differentiation between sexes did not exist at that point - it is a concept invented and created by the gods. This is yet another way in which Odin and his brothers polished and used the raw chaotic energy of Ymir. Even the name Ymir (the Screamer) alludes to the idea that the Aesir took a scream, a wordless means of communication, and transformed it into language, giving it an elevated form.

As with many other creation myths, the Norse

interpretation of the origin of the world is focused on the theme of conflict. Ymir is created as a result of the conflict between ice and fire. The world comes into being as a result of the sons of Bor killing and dismembering Ymir, the conflict between chaos and order. This primordial murder is not interpreted as a sin, as it would have been in a Biblical myth. The slaying of Ymir is a necessity, an act that had to be done for the sake of creating the world and bringing honor to the gods' name. This myth taught Vikings that they needed to do what it takes to garner a good reputation and that they should specifically engage in honorable aggressions.

The Norsemen believed that their gods were the forces that impaired sanctity and order into the world, and that held the cosmos together. This is why there are many stories about the gods interfering in Earthly affairs; it is their role to maintain order in the world, a role that would only end when the world itself would perish. But the Norse believed that giants too were able to intervene in the human world. Everything that was created came from Ymir and aspects of his, such as his ruggedness, his might, his fluctuating character, were still present in the world of mortals, despite the gods shaping all that existed to fit their personal agenda. For the Vikings, the conflict between the gods and the giants was a never-ending ordeal, and they, the humans, were right in the middle of it, presenting characteristics from both worlds: the order and honor of the gods but also the wickedness and chaos of the giants. The resolution of this fight will be Ragnarok, the end times, when all will be destroyed and nothing will remain of the old world. Then, a new world will rise from the seas, and the cycle of life will start again.

Mythology in Viking Society

Despite having a collection of stories through which we can look at a different side of Viking society, Norse mythology is a hard subject to pin down. In the Old Norse, they refer to it as *siour* (custom), and each individual declared their devotion to a deity that they connected to, on some personal level, and the worship of said god became an integral part of that person's life.

Norse gods were complex beings with distinct personalities, and many were venerated by entire communities. Scandinavian settlements had temples and places of worship where they would make sacrifices to garner the favor of the gods in times of war or celebrations. We don't know much about the exact rituals or customs they had, because much of their religion was passed down orally, from a generation to another, and not written. We should also keep in mind that the Norsemen were extremely flexible, even when it came to their traditions and worship. Their religion transformed with time and it had multiple variations across the vast Viking world. They shared the belief in the divine powers but each settlement assigned them their own functions and attributes. Even when they shifted to Christianity, Vikings remained polytheistic, mostly adding to the list of divine beings they believed in rather than replacing one with another.

Besides the families of gods and the giants, the Norse people also believed in *Disir* (female deities who were worshipped by specific families or individuals, kind of like the household deities of Roman, Greek, and other cultures), elves (who were separated into dark elves and light elves), dwarves, trolls, draugar (the undead), dragons and many other fantastic creatures. So it's a rich mythological world with plenty of supernatural beings, most of them representing certain fears or beliefs of the Norse population of that time.

With all being said, let's jump right into meeting the most powerful and important Norse gods and discover who they were and what they meant for the Norse people through their most iconic stories.

Chapter 4: The Aesir Gods

Most of the popular Norse gods belong to the Aesir family. In this chapter, we will cover some notable Aesir gods along with their iconic myths and their potential interpretations.

Odin the Allfather

Odin is regarded as the ruler of the Aesir gods, and he is one of the most complex characters in Norse mythology. He is attributed to a number of contradicting traits that make him a hard to understand deity, especially if we look at things from a Viking's perspective. Odin is both a god of war, justice, and law but also a selfish seeker of knowledge who dwells in poetry and doesn't care for communal values such as fairness. He is worshipped by those who look for honor and prestige but he is also a patron of the outlaws.

Even his name, *Odin* (the Master of Ecstasy) alludes to a unity between the multiple aspects of life respectively wisdom, war, magic (which is weird because as I mentioned before, Vikings had little respect for men who had magic abilities) poetry, sovereignty, and death. So, in what manners does Odin reflect these often contradicting aspects? Let's take them one by one and see.

War is perhaps the aspects that Odin is most predominantly linked with, in our modern portrayals of him. We often see him represented as an honorable commander, leading his armies into battle. But this portrayal is more suitable for deities such as Thor or Tyr. Odin, on the other hand, was adept at inciting strife between peaceful people, for his sheer enjoyment. He was, for the most part, concerned with the chaotic energy of war and the frenzy that came with it. As for those he affiliated himself with, Odin kept closer to rulers and berserkers, rather than the average warriors. Only the greatest fighters and heroes were deemed honorable enough to gain Odin's favors. As for the berserkers, they were special warriors who had the ability to tap into the spirits of ferocious beasts, such as bears and wolves, and use their power in battle. Since Odin too dabbled in shamanisms and other such spiritual practices, it's not hard to see why he was a patron of the warrior-shamans.

Sovereignty and leadership is another aspect that's closely tied in with Odin's identity, mostly because he is the archetypal ruler and the chief of the Aesir gods. So it was natural for the Norse chieftains and kings to claim themselves to be Odin's descendants or his protegees. But Odin is not the only Norse divinity associated with the Scandinavian rulers. Few know that Tyr was also a patron of kings, with the difference being that Tyr represented the lawful, virtuous, and just ruler while Odin was associated with cunning, devious, and inspired rulers. Let's not forget that Odin patronage outlaws, especially those who were exiled for heinous crimes. These men were strong-willed but they, just like Odin, defied societal norms. They were warriors but also poets at heart, and they sought to carve their own path into the world. The men that garnered Odin's favor were creative, intelligent, and unstoppable when it came to getting what they desired. Only luck and circumstances deemed them either rulers or outlaws. In fact, Odin's popularity among criminals is said to have led to his banishment from Asgard for ten years, because the other gods didn't want to be associated with his vile reputation. Thus, being a ruler that served Odin didn't always speak wonders of your character.

Wisdom and magic (or shamanism) are perhaps the two aspects that the Vikings attributed most frequently to the Allfather, and we seldom find them in modern portrayals of Odin. Unlike the Christian God, who is all-knowing, Norse deities are limited by their particularities. Odin makes no exception to this, which is why many stories of him present him in the role of a seeker, for wisdom, knowledge, and power (usually magical power). Odin is a driven individual who is ready to go the extra mile to surpass his limitations. In Norse legends, Odin is always on the look for new means of gaining knowledge and power. He speaks to wise people, he uses his two ravens, Munin (Memory) and Hugin (Thought), to gather news about what's happening around the realms of Norse mythology, and his throne, Hlidskialf, lets him see everything that's going on, without him having to leave Asgard. His desire to know all there is to be known also stems from his dread for the ever-approaching Ragnarok when he is doomed to perish alongside the other gods. Let's see the iconic Norse myths that speak of Odin's thirst for knowledge.

Odin's Sacrifice to Learn the Magic of the Runes

The story of how Odin learned the magic spells from the rules is rather well-known. It is said that Odin pierced himself with his own spear, Gungnir, and hung himself from a branch of the World Tree, Yggdrasill, above the Well of Urd (that was guarded by the Norns) to garner the wisdom of the runes. You see, only the dead to those who were deemed worthy by the Well of Urd were allowed to learn the magic of the runes, so he put a noose around his head and he hung himself for nine days and nine nights, managing to learn nine spells - a great accomplishment considering that he allegedly only saw the runes for a split second before falling from the branch. The number nine has a special significance, and it is mostly associated with magic. During his time in the tree, Odin forbade any deity to aid him in any way.

The ninth night is when Odin ritually died. All light extinguished to mark the god's death and the magical powers of the spirit world reached their peak. The last night of the ritual coincided with the celebration of Walpurgis Night when large bonfires are lit to celebrate this moment of great power. Odin's death was however short-lasting, and after midnight the light returned to the world, and with it the Allfather who now knew the mighty spells of the runes as well as how to perform incredible feats. For example, Odin learned how to heal all wounds, to wake the dead, to free himself from any type of constraints, to win and keep the love of anyone, and many other things. With this knowledge, he became one of the wisest beings in the Universe.

Thematically speaking, Odin's sacrifice is of himself to himself, and his lower self (that died) to his higher self (the Odin who gained more knowledge, becoming a better version of himself) ringing true to that selfish sense of individuality characteristic of Viking civilization.

Odin and the Well of Mimir

The Well of Mimir, most commonly referred to as the Well of Knowledge, was near Yggdrasill's root that extended over to Jotunheim (the world of the frost giants) and it was guarded by Mimir. He was the wisest of the Aesir gods, specifically because he often drank from the Well of Knowledge. But the price he requested out of those who wanted to gain knowledge was not cheap. Heimdall, the Norse god who guards the Bifrost (the rainbow bridge that links Asgard to Midgard) had to give up one of his earlobes to drink from the well and Mimir didn't make any special offers for the ruler of the Aesir. On the contrary, he asked for one of Odin's eyes. It is unknown whether Odin immediately accepted or bargained for a more suitable deal, but in the end, he did sacrifice his eye, becoming the One-Eyed-God.

The fact that Odin's sacrifice is one of his eyes is a meaningful detail. The eye was always seen as a symbol and metaphor, both in poems and in everyday expressions. It is the window of the soul and the physical representation of one's perception of the world. Here, it seems like the latter concept is more suitable, meaning that Odin traded the way he saw the world for wisdom, which allows for a different perception. For Odin, this trade must have seemed fair, since for him all that mattered was to become his "higher self" and gain the wisdom of the divine.

In a separate myth about one of the numerous Aesir-Vanir wars, Mimir's head is cut off and sent to Odin. The Vanirs felt cheated when they were given Vili as an advisor, only to find out that he wasn't very bright and all his good advice was actually from Mimir. Vili was Odin's brother so they didn't dare to touch him, but Mimir was fair game. Odin however, was not one to waste a good opportunity. Mimir was, after all, the wisest of the gods. When he received Mimir's head he embalmed it, with his special herbs so it would not decay. Then, he used one of the spells he learned from the runes to bring Mimir's head back to life. From then on, Odin would often use Mimir's advice in times of need. This is yet another way in which Mimir provided Odin with knowledge, albeit we could argue that Mimir got the short end of the stick here, becoming a talking head and all.

Magic and Poetry

Odin and Freya are the greatest shamans of the Norse gods. Shamanism is a form of magic in which practitioners can contact spirits or interact with the spirit world to accomplish a purpose. Odin is especially known for his spiritual-journeys, while his body remained in Asgard, appearing to others as if he was asleep. Such an instance is when he visited the underworld, on Sleipnir (an eight-legged horse attributed to shamanic trances) to find out what was Baldur's fate. As a practitioner of shamanism, Odin is surrounded by plenty of animal familiar spirits, such as his ravens, the wolves Geri and Fleki, and even the Valkyries (even though they are maidens, they are still spiritual beings that serve the Allfather). The ritual of death and rebirth that Odin underwent in order to decipher the runes is also part of shamanic practice, if there was any doubt left regarding the god's abilities.

Shamanism is a part of the traditional *seidr,* the form of magic that was considered acceptable for only women to master - that is why Freya is a patron of it. Men who practiced seidr were scorned and even banished from society if the animosities ran deep. Odin's affinity for shamanism made him a target for ridicule and taunts. His 10-years exile from Asgard is said to have been in part due to his preferences in "doing a woman's work." To say that magic tarnished Odin's reputation would be an understatement. It questioned his honor and his ability to perform his "manly" duties. However, to Odin, the idea of honor was not everything, and he gladly discarded the concept if it meant he could indulge in ecstatic practices.

Odin's connection to poetry goes back to the time when he stole the mead of poetry, a drink made by the dwarves from Kvasir's corpse. Kvasir was the wisest man to ever live, and anyone who consumed the mead made from his body gained knowledge and the ability to compose poems. Of course, Odin was interested in possessing this mead, and he acquired it through trickery; by seducing the giantess who guarded it. But Odin, in an act of generosity, decided to share the gift of poetry with humans, gods, and other beings, making him a patron of scholars, poets, storytellers, and composers. To flaunt his poetic abilities, it is said that Odin only speaks through verses.

Death

We may not think of Odin as a god of death, but the Vikings clearly believed him to be deeply connected to the dead. He is, after all, the one who presides over Valhalla, the Viking Heaven, and a fine connoisseur of the spiritual world. His ability to speak and interact with the dead makes him sort of a necromancer, although his purpose is solely to garner as much knowledge as he can.

Perhaps to honor this aspect of Odin, his worship consisted of frequent human sacrifices, especially notable ones such as enemy rulers or nobles. These sacrifices were accomplished with the use of a noose or a spear, elements that allude to Odin's self-sacrifice to learn the magic of the runes. Although Odin is not the stereotypical Norse god or a personification of the Viking ideals, he is the vital force of all vital forces and the ruler of all gods. He represents inspiration, fury, ecstasy, selfishness, and the drive to accomplish the goals he has set for himself, regardless of how others might judge him for it.

Odin presides over the most fundamental aspects of a Viking's life, and for that, even though he was fundamentally flawed, he was the most worshipped and honored of all Norse deities. A far cry from our idea of a ruler of the gods, but at least he was a relatable figure that the Norsemen could connect with on a deeper level.

Thor the God of Thunder

Thor is the son of Odin and one of the most prominent deities in Norse mythology. He is the ideal Viking warrior, a role model for all young Norsemen, sporting virtues such as honor and unshakable loyalty. These qualities come in handy because he is the defendant of Asgard, protecting the gods from the ever-present threat of giants and whatever enemies might come their way. No one can measure in strength with Thor, and to double up his forces he wears a special belt of power and yields the famous hammer Mjolnir (Lightning) that never misses and always comes back to his owner. Whenever there was a lightning storm, the old Scnaidnavians believed that it was Thor battling with the giants in Asgard, as he rode in his chariot drawn by goats. As a side note here, the Vikings didn't believe that Thor was actually riding in a chariot pulled by real goats, they are just a symbol for the invisible and incomprehensible world of the gods. Many elements in Norse mythology are not meant to be taken literally.

Although Thor is the greatest slayer of giants and, subsequently the greatest keeper of peace and order, he is ironically described as having giant proportions and coming from a giant ancestry. Let's not forget that Odin is half-giant, and Thor's mother, Jord, is of pure giant blood. This is just to show that relationships between the gods and the giants were not as simple as we'd like to believe, and many gods were in some way or another of giant lineage. Nevertheless, Thor's greatest foe is Jumurgandr, the great sea serpent that's coiled around the human world. It is said that the two will face each other at Ragnarok when both will day of the other's "hands."

The Creation of Mjolnir

The story of how Thor got his favorite weapon is quite funny. It all started with Loki, the god of mischief, who, on a particularly boring day decided to pull a prank on Sif, Thor's wife, and cut her beautiful golden locks. Understandably, Thor didn't appreciate Loki's sense of humor, and he threatened to break every bone in Loki's body if he didn't fix the situation. The trickster god pleaded for his life, and he came up with the idea to go and ask for the help of the crafty dwarves. Surely, they would find a way to give Sif a new head of golden hair.

In Svartalfheim, the home of the dwarves, Loki found what he was looking for, but he also managed to get himself into even more trouble. You see, he first approached the sons of Ivaldi and told them that the gods were holding a contest to see who could create the most marvelous gifts. They crafted Sif's hair, alongside two other great artifacts: Gungnir that would become Odin's spear, and Skidbladnir, the greatest ship in the world, that was gifted to Freyr. Loki however, also approached the dwarven brothers Brokkr and Sindri, and he taunted them saying that they could never create marvels as incredible as those of the sons of Ivaldi. The brothers took the bait, on one condition - if the gods preferred their gifts, Brokkr and Sindri would receive Loki's head. Against his better judgment, Loki accepted the wager, but he was also not adept at playing fair. To sabotage the brothers, he transformed himself into a fly and he pestered Brokkr who tended to the fire while Sindri worked on the gifts.

Despite Loki's involvement, the first two pieces ended up being flawless. The first marvel was Gullinbursti, a boar with golden hair, who was faster than any horse and who lit up in the dark - he was gifted to Freyr, the god of the harvest. The second wonder was Draupnir, a magic ring that would create eight golden rings of similar weight and value every nine nights (again notice the use of number nine in relation to magic). This ring of wealth went to Odin, the Allfather. But for the third marvel, Loki's sabotage prevailed, and Mjolnir, the greatest hammer to ever exist, ended up having a rather short handle. Sindri and Brokkr were unhappy with the hammer, but they were still pretty confident in the quality of their gifts, so they made their way to Asgard to present them to the gods.

The gods were extremely happy with everything they got. Sif had recovered her wonderful golden hair, Freyr had two new tools to help him complete his duties, Odin had a mighty weapon and a ring that produced him more wealth, and Thor had the perfect item to help him smite giants - he couldn't care less about the short handle. To Loki's horror, Brokkr and Sindri were declared winners, and they were eager to claim their prize. But Loki was as clever as he was devious, and he pointed out that he had not promised them his neck, thus there was no way for them to take his head. The dwarves then decided to sew Loki's mouth shut, and they returned to Svartalfheim empty-handed but content. That is the story of how Thor got his hammer, a myth that speaks more of Loki's character than of Thor's.

Thor's Role in the Viking Society

Besides his role as a divine guardian, Thor is known for his activities in the human realm. He was called upon whenever there was a need for protection, comfort, and purification, especially of a place or event. The hammer, Mjolnir, is said to have had both smiting and blessing powers (in the sense that it destroyed evil forces), and many runic inscriptions that speak about Thor invoke him to bless places, plots of lands, and weddings. A peculiar demonstration of Thor's ability to purify and bless is the myth of him eating his goats and blessing their hides with his hammer to bring them back to life.

Thor's association with agriculture and fertility, in general, comes from him being a sky god - one that could invoke rain as he pleased. Historians believe that his golden-haired wife Sif was a personification of good harvest, her locks symbolizing fields of grains, thus their marriage being a portrayal of prosperity through the union of the divine spirits of the sky and those of the Earth.

But Thors's principal role in the Viking society remains that of a role model for warriors. If we add his affinity to the farming class to the mix, it is not hard to see why Thor was such a beloved god for the Norsemen. In many ways, Thor is the perfect opposite of Odin. He is the god of the common people and the fighters, and he values honesty and loyalty. This is why Thor's popularity skyrocketed throughout the Viking Age, to the point that he surpassed Odin, with the most telling example of this preference being the Icelandic Viking colony. The Norsemen of Iceland venerated Thor, in part because they were mainly a farming settlement, but also because they had experienced first-hand the oppressions of the noble class (who happened to worship Odin). To farmers, settlers, and colonists, Thor is seen as a protector and a true leader, one that rules with honor and blesses his people.

Thor's cult also saw a peak when Christianity first came to the Scandinavian world. This new religion sought to annihilate the traditions and beliefs of the Norsemen, and Thor became a symbol of hostility towards these invading forces. Vikings of that time who refused to give up on the old gods would wear pendants brandished to resemble miniature hammers - small Mjolnirs, to show their allegiances, a retaliation to the cross amulets worn by Christians.

Loki the Trickster God

Loki is a very peculiar character of Norse mythology, with a similarly strange lineage. His father, Farbauti, is a giant and his mother, Laufey, is of unspecified descent in Norse lore. She could have been a giant, a god, or even a human. Loki himself has fathered a complicated family. His proper wife was Sigyn, a goddess of victory, with whom he had a son called Narfi. But Loki also had an entanglement with the giantess Angrboda, with whom he had three children, Hel, Fenrir, and Jumungandr, each being more monstrous and destructive than the other. Jumungandr and Fenrir alone have rather prominent roles to play at Ragnarok, and Hel is the goddess of the underworld.

Leaving his perplexing family ties aside, Loki is a deity that defies most Viking societal norms. He has little to no regard for his fellow gods, he is malicious, cowardly, extremely selfish, and almost every action he takes is with self-preservation and mischief in mind. Loki also defies the laws of nature in an instance by being the mother of Sleipnir, the shamanic horse with eight legs. That was possible when he turned himself into a mare to seduce Svadilfari's stallion, stopping him from winning a bet with the gods that would have granted him the sun, the moon, and the goddess Freya as a bride. We've already seen Loki's character in the Creation of Mjolnir, but another story that speaks volumes about his treacherous character and his lack of loyalty towards any faction is that of the Kidnapping of Idun.

The Kidnapping of Idun

Idun is a primordial goddess of Norse mythology, and she is the keeper of the fruits of immortality, which allow gods to remain young and strong. Whenever a god felt like they were starting to age, they would go to Idun and she entrusted them one fruit- that was enough to ward off old age and give them their youth back. So, what happened to her?

Well, one day, Loki, Odin, and Hoenir went on a perilous journey. There was little to eat in the desolate regions they traveled through, but they managed to find an ox and kill it. But no matter how long they kept the meat over the fire, it wouldn't cook. It turns out that Thjazi, a giant, was using magic to prevent them from cooking their meat, and he wanted a piece of the ox for himself in exchange for letting them prepare their dinner. The gods reluctantly agreed, but when the giant came down, taking the form of an eagle, and snatched the biggest, juiciest piece of meat, Loki got angry. He launched a thick branch at the eagle, but Thjazi fought back and took Loki to the sky. Loki, terrified that Thjazi would drop him, pleaded for his life, and the giant relented. But his price was high, to say the least. He wanted Idun and her fruits of immortality.

Loki spent what remained of the journey thinking of a plan to trick Idun into being captured by Thjazi. Of course, he found a way. He told her that he had seen incredible fruits - yes, even more, incredible than hers, beyond the walls of Asgard, and that he would bring her to these fruits if she wanted to compare them by herself. Poor Idun was fooled, and when they reached the wood she was taken by Thjazi, to his abode situated in the highest mountain peak of Jotunheim. Without Idun and her fruits, the gods grew old and sick. They quickly discovered that Loki was behind the goddess's disappearance and they threatened to kill him if he didn't retrieve her. Loki then took Freya's hawk feather cape, which allowed him to turn into a hawk and he flew to Jotunheim.

He was lucky enough to find Idun alone and unsupervised, and he wasted no time. He turned her into a nut and flew back to Asgard with her in his talons. But Loki didn't make it back home before Thjazi found out, and he turned into an eagle and caught up with the treacherous god. Fortunately for Loki, the gods from Asgard were on the lookout and they built a wooden barrier around Asgard. After Loki made it back, they lit the barrier, killing Thjazi who didn't have time to turn back and plunged right into the flames. However, the story doesn't end there. Skadi, Thjazi's daughter soon came to Asgard to demand restitution for the murder of her father. Her request was for the gods to make her laugh because the death of her father had saddened her deeply.

Loki, the trickster god, was the only one who could accomplish such a feat. He tied one end of a rope around his male parts and the other one around a goat's beard, creating an absurd spectacle that even the frost giant couldn't gaze at without laughing. That is how Loki both caused and solved Idun's kidnapping and how he made up for the death of Thjazi to his daughter, Skadi.

The Deity Without a Cult

There are countless legends in which Loki commits crimes against the gods, and he ultimately pays for his wrongdoings. To punish him, the gods tie him down, with his legitimate son's entrails, to three rocks. The number three is sacred in Norse myths, and it is usually linked to royalty and divinity. In this case, it signifies Loki's divine punishment. It is said that a poisonous snake sits above Loki, dripping poison in his eyes. Sigyn, his wife, stays by his side and holds a bowl above his face, to catch the poison. But every once in a while the bowl gets full and she has to go and empty it while Loki writhes in agony. Loki will be freed at Ragnarok, to witness the end of the world at the hands of his children (mostly Fenrir).

Loki's identity was questioned by the many Scandinavian tribes. Some recognized him as a god, others considered him a giant, and a few cults believed him to be a different kind of mythological being. Similarly, there is confusion regarding the meaning of his name. If we go by the popular theory that Loki means *tangle* or *knot* then that is very telling of his character. His schemes tangle the deities in dangerous situations, and he himself can be considered the knot or the flaw in the cosmos that causes the end of the world. What's certain is that Loki is a traitor, a schemer, and a complete antithesis of the traditional Viking values. Thus it is to no surprise that, as far as we know, there was no cult or following around him. There is no record speaking of Loki worshippers, nor of celebrations or sacrifices in his name. So, ironically, Loki is one of the most important characters of Norse legends and the element that causes or triggers most Norse myths, but there is no worship or cult around him. In the end, it seems that Loki's biggest joke was himself.

Baldur the Beloved God

Baldur is the son of Odin and Frigg, and he is the deity beloved by all beings and creatures that have a physical form. He is often described as being handsome and cheerful, but his name which roughly translates as "bold" also alludes to Baldur's war-like character. The most well-known myth about Baldur is that of his death.

The Death of the Beloved God

The story starts with an ode to Baldur's character and how much he was appreciated by the other gods for his ability to bring joy to anyone's heart. But, at some point, the young god starts to have ominous dreams about his death, making everybody in Asgard worry about his fate. The gods appointed Odin to look into the matter and find out what Baldur's dreams meant. And so he did. Odin disguised himself, took Sleipnir, and embarked on one of his shamanic journeys to the underworld where he knew of a wise seeress who could clarify the matter. When he got to the cold realm of Niflheim he was surprised to see the halls decorated, as if some great celebration was about to occur. He hurried to the seeress and inquired her about the preparations only to find that the distinguished guest for whom all the underworld was decorated was no other than Baldur.

Odin returned to Asgard and shared the sorrowful news. That's where Frigg, a devout mother, stepped in. She was prepared to do anything to potentially spare her son from this horrible fate. In a desperate attempt, she went to all the living and nonliving things in the universe and extracted an oath for them, to not harm Baldur. Frigg was very thorough in her mission but she made a fatal mistake - she skipped the mistletoe. To her, the small plant looked harmless, and there was no point in asking. Surely, there was no way that the mistletoe would bring any harm to her beloved son. When Loki got wind of this, he saw the opportunity for mischief.

While all the other gods made somewhat of a sport out of Baldur's invulnerability, by throwing rocks and sticks at him and laughing when they bounced off, leaving no wound behind, Loki got to scheming. He carved a spear out of mistletoe and he approached Hodr, the blind god, with apparent kindness. Loki told Hodr that he understood that he felt left out and he offered to help him take part in the game and honor Baldur's invincibility. The trickster handed Hodr the mistletoe spear and he guided his hands in the right direction. All Hodr had to do was throw, and throw he did. The weapon pierced Baldur, killing him in an instant. Poor Hodr who just wanted to fit in was nothing but a pawn in Loki's game.

The gods remained still at the sight of Baldur's corpse, not just because they cared deeply for the god, but also due to the fact that his death was foreseen in the first presage of Ragnarok. Frigg was the first to snap out of the stupor and look for a solution. The only chance that Baldur had left was for someone to go to the underworld and bargain with Hel, the goddess of the death, for his release. Hermod, a brother of Baldur took on the challenge. He borrowed Sleipnir from Odin and off he went to the realm of the dead, while the other gods prepared a worthy funeral for their dear friend. Beings from all the nine realms attended this ceremony, from gods to giants, dwarves, elves, humans and even valkyries gathered to mourn the death of Baldur.

They turned Hringhorni, Baldur's ship, into a funeral pyre and they attempted to launch it into the sea. When the ship didn't bulge, they called for Hyrrokkin, the strongest giantess, to free Hringhorni from the sand. The giantess managed to launch the ship to sea, but Nanna, Baldur's wife, couldn't bear the sight of her husband being carried to his last voyage and she died of sorrow. They place her body next to Baldur's and then Thor lit the flames. As sacrifices, Odin placed his ring Draupnir in the flames, and Baldur's horse was led in the fire, to follow his master in the afterlife.

Hermod's journey took nine nights (the divine number) but he made it to Hel. The half-living, half-dead goddess of the underworld was a strange sight, and her popularity as a harsh and greedy deity did not honor her. And there, sitting in a chair next to Loki's monstrous daughter was Baldur, or what had remained of him - a pale and lifeless spirit who looked nothing like the joyous deity. Hermod pleaded for Baldur's life, telling

Hel that all the living things in the world missed him deeply. Hel was not a cruel goddess, so she presented Hermod with a deal. If the gods could determine that all the living things wept for Baldur, the living world would get him back. If, however, even one being did not care for Baldur's demise, he would remain in the underworld, forever. Hermod hurried home with the good news, and the gods wasted no time in sending messengers to find out if everything wept for Baldur. And they all did, except for one giantess called Tokk, who showed no sympathy towards Baldur's fate. Tokk was none other than Loki himself, determined to see his devious plan to the very end.

Thus Baldur was doomed to remain in the underworld, and his joyous and glorious light never graced the land of the living again.

Baldur's Character

Although in his most famous legend Baldur plays a passive role, we should not forget that he is a Norse god, who adheres to Viking ideals of a role model. In different sources that mention him, Baldur is presented as a deity that's always eager to engage in war and lead others to battle, making him a similar figure to Thor, albeit on a much smaller scale. Baldur never quite matched Thor's popularity, and because most of the sources that speak of Norse mythology are fragmentary in nature, we don't know a great deal about Baldur. What we do know is that the Vikings held him in high regard, for both his joyous personality and his war-like attributes, and they honored the memory of the beloved god of Asgard.

Tyr the God of War and Justice

When we think of important Norse deities, Tyr is not the first god to pop into our minds. He, like Baldur, is not present in many myths and legends, but it is widely believed that he was once one of the most cherished deities in the Norse pantheon, for his role as a war god and protector of justice. In epic poems, Norse heroes such as Sigurd, often invoke Tyr to garner victories in battles. Additionally, the part he plays in the story of the Binding of Fenrir, speaks volume of his just and heroic character.

The Binding of Fenrir, Son of Loki

Fenrir the wolf is the third son of Loki and the giantess Angrboda. Just as with his brothers, the gods had terrible premonitions regarding Fenrir's fate. He is said to be the one who will devour Odin at Ragnarok, allowing chaos to reign free and destroy the cosmos. Out of all Loki's monstrous children, the gods feared Fenrir the most, so they took him while he was still a pup to grow in

Asgard, under their watchful eyes. The deity who took upon himself the responsibility to feed and care for the infant wolf was Tyr, the most honorable of the gods.

As weeks turned into months, Fenrir grew bigger and bigger, and the Norse deities understood that they had little time to find a way to contain the beast. They attempted to bind him with various chains, by tricking Fenrir into believing that they were but challenges to test his strength. With each chain that the beast shattered, the gods cheered to not garner the wolf's suspicion, but their anxiety grew with every failure. Finally, in the last attempt, the gods asked for the dwarves' help. They were, after all, the greatest craftsmen in the nine realms, surely they could create a chain that could bind even the fearsome Fenrir. This final attempt proved successful when the dwarves created Gleipnir, a chain made out of things that don't exist, such as the beard of a woman and a fish's breath.

But Gleipnir was a light and dainty-looking chain, and upon seeing it Fenrir suspected foul play. The wolf beast was not stupid, he agreed to try the chain only if a god or goddess would put their hand in his mouth, as a symbol of good faith. Of course, no deity rushed to fulfill Fenrir's demand, as it meant losing a limb. And yet Tyr, the brave, volunteered to put his hand in the wolf's jaw, for the sake of the world. You'd think that Fenrir would have a moment of hesitation to bite the proverbial hand that fed him, but he didn't. When he realized the gods' treachery, he chomped off Tyr's hand in an instant. Fenrir's story ends with him being tied to a boulder and transported to some sordid place. There, with a sword in his jaws to hold his mouth open, Fenrir awaits for Ragnarok, when he will be freed to carry out his destiny.

This myth is the most telling portrayal of Tyr as a divine upholder of the law. He sacrifices his hand not only to save the world from Fenrir's threat but also to offer just compensation for the gods not maintaining their side of the oath. His act fulfills the deities' end of the bargain, bringing justness and order to this whole affair. This instance mimics that of Odin sacrificing his eye for wisdom, showing that he is the foremost deity of wisdom, with the difference that, through his sacrifice, Tyr proves that he is the greatest god of justice and law.

Tyr's Roles in the Norse World

It might seem weird that a god of justice is also one of war, but for the Vikings, these two aspects were deeply entwined. From the Norsemen's point of view, war was not simply a chaotic bloody business, but somewhat of a lawful duel, where the gods decided who won and who was defeated. In many cases, the dates and places of the battles were chosen beforehand by both armies, and the Vikings had precise rules in place to prevent good war conduct. Similarly, the law could sometimes be used to gain victory over an enemy, just like war, so it makes sense to have the same deity handling both law and war.

Even though there are few surviving records of Tyr, it is clear that he was, at some point, a cherished deity of justice, before whom people swore oaths, but also a patron of honorable warriors. His worshippers valued him deeply and considered him to be on par with the mighty Thor and Odin, the ruler of the sky. It goes to show that if a deity of the time wanted the people's respect, all they had to do was sacrifice their hands to a monster of destruction that would one day bring the end of the world. Tough crowd, right?

Bites of Aesir Gods

Because few written accounts of Norse myths and legends have survived through the ages, there are plenty of Viking deities that we know little about - so little that I don't even have enough information to give them their own separate subchapter here. So, instead of allowing these gods to be forgotten, here are some "bites of the Norse gods" with some interesting things we know about the more obscure Aesir deities.

Heimdall

Heimdall is the son of Odin and the guardian of Asgard, who sits at the top of the Bifrost. He is said to have keen eyesight and hearing, which he uses to detect potential intruders. Heimdall holds the horn Gjallarhorn, which will ultimately signal the arrival of giants at Ragnarok. Heimdall's biggest enemy is Loki, and they are destined to kill each other at the end of the world, much like Jumungandr and Thor. Some Old Norse poems speak of Heimdall as being the one who created mankind and established the Viking society. An interesting fact about the guardian of Asgard is that he was born from nine different mothers, a miraculous feat to say the least.

Vili and Ve

Vili and Ve are Odin's brothers, and they are credited both for the construction of the universe and for the creation of the first two humans (both feats were done in collaboration with the Allhather). Despite being founding deities, there are few mentions of Odin's two brothers in myths and poems, except for a small note that they had slept with Frigg during Odin's 10 years of exile. Even so, they must have been extremely important to the Vikings at some point for their simple kinship to the ruler of the Aesir if for nothing else. In the Old Norse, Vili roughly translates to "will" and Ve to "temple," suggesting that the pair were associated with the sacred and the holy. Other interpretations are that the three brothers represent the basic forces that distinguish the existing world from chaos, respectively inspiration, intention, consciousness, and the sacred.

Some Old Norse texts allude to the fact that Vili and Ve are nothing more than different representations of Odin, a theory that complicates the family ties of the Aesir gods.

Ullr

Ullr was the son of Sif, and he is said to have been a great hunter and archer. Although he is an obscure deity, some surviving accounts of him describe Ullr as being a handsome war-deity, who was frequently invoked before duels. The mention of "Ullr's Blessing" in an epic poem suggests that Ullr was a deity of great importance in the Norse pantheon. His name can be translated as either "temple" tying him to the sacred, or "glory" linking him furthermore with war and war-like abilities. Some historians suggest that Ullr was a deity of law and justice, connecting him with Tyr, but there is little to no evidence to prove this supposed link. Other theories are that Ullr was actually part of the Vanir tribe, because there is a mention of him crossing the sea at some point, and many Vanir deities were associated with the iconography of water. But that is also just another theory about the enigmatic son of Sif.

Hoenir

Hoenir is another god with an enigmatic existence. He is often portrayed as the travel companion of Odin and Loki, but most accounts about him are confusing, to say the least. In some stories, he is credited with having a role in the creation of Ask and Embla, the first humans, while other legends speak of him as if he is an extension or identity of Odin (mostly because ecstasy was his gift). Hoenir is described as being a swift god, a fearful deity, and a handsome man. In fact, during an Aesir-Vanir war, when he and Mimir were offered as hostages from the Aesir, the Vanir were taken aback by Hoenir's beauty and they made him their chieftain. The rest you already know, although in that story Hoenir was replaced with Vili; the Vanir discovered how dim-witted Hoenir was and in a rage, they decapitated Mimir and sent his head to Odin, as a retaliation. But this characterization of Hoenir being a timid and dim-witted deity is contradictory to other portrayals in which he resembles Odin in abilities and characteristics. Was Hoenir nothing more than a pretty face or was he a powerful and important Norse deity? We'll probably never know.

Chapter 5: The Vanir Gods

There is a lot of debate when it comes to the Aesir-Vanir classification of the Norse gods. What sets the Vanir apart from the Aesir is a tendency towards having a closer connection to mankind and their affinity for agriculture as a whole. But even these attributes aren't always singular to Vanir gods. Take Thor, for example. Besides his roles as guardian and warrior, he is also a god of fertility and harvest, and his connection with the Viking people is perhaps one of the most significant out of all Norse deities. And yet, he is undeniably an Aesir god. Additionally, the word "Vanir" is rarely used in Old Norse texts that precede the Christian conversion of Vikings. So, at the end of the day, the whole Aesir-Vanir matter is pretty confusing.

Regardless of the controversies, three deities are commonly assigned to the Vanir family: Freya, Freyr, and Njord. According to Norse myths, they lived in Vanaheim (the realm of the Vanir), a place that is said to have been closer to nature than Asgard but still within the Aesir realm territory. The existence and descriptions of Vanaheim are just disputed in the historical world as those of the Vanir family.

Freya

Freya is one of the most important Norse goddesses, and the most prominent Vanir deity (although she became an honorary Aesir after an Aesir-Vanir war). She is the sister of Freyr and the wife of Odr, a god of inspiration and ecstasy. Freya is frequently portrayed as being beautiful, joyous, gentle, and very fond of material possessions as well as the elusive concept of love. Many stories speak of her romantic endeavors with other gods and creatures of the Norse mythology, including elves. But let's not forget that to Asgard and the old Norsemen, Freya was much more than a fun-loving deity with a fondness for the finer things in life. She is the goddess who presides over Folkvang, the afterlife realm for unmarried maidens, and one of the greatest practitioners of seidr (and the one who brought magic to gods and humans alike).

I mentioned seidr a lot throughout this book, but I never took the time to explain its nature. It is a form of magic combined with shamanism, that serves the purpose of finding out the course of one's fate and changing it by adding new events. Thus seidr could be used in a great number of ways. In the Viking Age, the women who practiced seidr were known as *vola*, and they would perform acts of magic in exchange for goods, food, or accommodation. The Vikings' sentiments towards volas were mixed. They respected them and celebrated them, but they also feared them and treated them as outcasts. In the historic period that preceded the Viking Age, it was customary for a war chief's wife to be a practitioner of seidr, and her role was to foresee and influence the outcome of a plan of action through her magic.

How Freya's beauty Led to Mjolin's Theft

The most popular stories of Freya revolve around her beauty. She was often the object of desire for antagonists, such as the giant Svaldifari who wanted to marry her (and get the moon and the sun) in exchange for building an impregnable wall around Asgard. Thankfully for her, Loki took one for the team and sabotaged Svaldifari by seducing his horse.

But another, more mainstream legend that speaks volumes of her reputation as a rare beauty is that of the theft of Mjolnir. The story goes that one day, Thor woke up to find that his precious hammer was gone. This was bad news for Asgard since without his weapon Thor couldn't fight off potential giant attacks. Freya lent Thor and Loki her falcon fathers to look for Mjolnir, and they quickly deduced that the perpetrator was Thrym, a giant. When confronted about the theft, Thrym made no effort to hide his crime, and he had the insolence to ask for something in return. Of course, this wouldn't be a story about Freya's beauty if the giant hadn't asked for her hand in marriage. The gods of Asgard, especially Freya, were livid, and they gathered to find a solution. The proposed plan quickly turned this otherwise classic myth of honorable gods versus the treacherous giants into a quirky legend: Thor was to disguise himself as Freya and go to the realm of giants to attend the wedding and get back his hammer. Somehow, all the gods agreed that was the best course of action.

And so Thor, dressed in a bridal gown, and Loki, disguised as his maid of honor, made their way to Jotunheim. At the welcome feast, Thor almost gave himself away with his insatiable appetite and his piercing gaze, but thankfully Loki was there to find unbelievable explanations that mitigated Thrym's suspicions. Then, at the ceremony,

Mjolin was brought to bless the union, as the traditional custom required. But when the hammer got to Thor, he took it and wasted no time to slay his groom along with all the wedding attendees. Thor then returned home with his precious weapon and all was, once again, well and good in Asgard.

Freya or Frigg

Although most sources present Freya and Frigg as being distinct deities, many elements connect the two. For one, Freya's husband, Odr, is virtually Odin. The names themselves are a dead giveaway (Odin and Odr have the same root) but Odr's association with inspiration and ecstasy is truly the nail in the proverbial coffin. There is even a story that portrays Freya as being Odin's concubine. If we also take into account the tales that speak of Odr's frequent journeys, it becomes very evident that Odr and Odin are the same deities, or at least that Odr is an extension of

Odin. That in exchange means that Freya and Frigg are either the same goddess or different sides of the same deity.

Let's not forget that Frigg herself had somewhat of a bad reputation of being an arduous lover, who even went as low as sleeping with Odin's brothers while he was exiled from Asgard. That sounds pretty similar to Freya's tales of romantic endeavors. Additionally, Frigg is frequently associated with the practice of magic, which comes to light through her proficiency in weaving and her extensive knowledge of the fate of all beings. The names of the two goddesses are also very peculiar. Freya or *Freyja* roughly translates to "lady" which sounds more like a social title than a name. Meanwhile, Frigg in the Old Norse meant "beloved," tying her to attributes such as love and desire, which are frequently used in portrayals of Freya. So in a weird twist, Frigg's name describes Freya's identity, while Freya's name describes just a social status rather than a unique characterization.

No matter how we look at this, it's impossible to not conclude that Freya and Frigg are ultimately the same people. Their husbands, their use of magic, their portrayal as sensual women, and their significance in the Norse pantheon, make it crystal clear that they share an identity. And yet, in many myths and legends they are portrayed as different individuals, one the Allmother and one a Vanir goddess of magic and fertility. Where is this separation coming from and what purpose does it serve? Unfortunately, we have no way of knowing that.

Freyr

Freyr is a god of peace, masculinity, good weather, and prosperity. He is Freya's twin and one of the most beloved deities of the common Norsemen who were farmers and settlers. Since his blessings were usually good harvest, fertility, prosperity, and health, it's not hard to understand why he was held in high regard and was often the recipient of sacrifices, especially during harvest festivals and weddings. Fortunately, his sacrifices were often boars and not humans, because that was Freyr's favorite animal, perhaps in reference to Gullinborsti - the golden bristled boar he had received from the dwarves Sindri and Brokkr.

Although he is a Vanir god and an honorary Aesir, Freyr lives in Alfheim, the realm of the elves. That could mean that he was a ruler of the elves or he had deep connections with the elusive creatures. Freyr is also known for his famous ship, Skidbladnir, that could be easily folded to fit in a bag and that always had a favorable wind. Skidbladnir is considered to symbolize the ritual ships used by the Scandinavian people during funeral rites or celebrations and not their longships. For on land transport, Freys is said to have used a chariot drawn by boars, his preferred beasts. During harvest celebrations, Freyr worshippers would put a statue of the god in a chariot and travel through the lands with it. All the settlements would welcome the procession and the festivities would ensure, overseen by the kind and peaceful presence of Freyr (or at least his statue).

We can understand the magnitude of Freyr's importance for the Norse people simply by the amount of information that we have regarding his worship and cult. As you've probably noticed by now, not much is known about the spiritual life of the Vikings, and yet for Freyr, we have details regarding not only sacrifices but also celebrations in his name. That's pretty huge! On top of that, the deity is credited with being the founding father of numerous royal lines and tribes.

Freyr's Wedding

The most well-known and one of the only surviving stories of Freyr is that of his marriage to the giantess Gerdr. It's a touching myth of how Freyr one day saw the woman of his dreams when he sat on Hlithskjolf, Odin's throne. Freyr then was overcome with sadness, because he couldn't be with that fair woman. His father, Njord noticed his son's depression and sent a servant, Skirnir, to tend to his needs. Freyr told Skirnir about his plight and he implored him to find Gerdr and ask for her hand in his name. Skirnir accepted the task but he asked for something in return - Freyr's magical sword, that fought on its own. Freyr complied and soon enough he and Gerdr met for the first time and they became a happy couple.

The myth is sweet in nature, but Freyr's sacrifice was perhaps bigger than what he bargained for. Without his sword, Freyr encountered many hardships in fights with various giants. It is said that at Ragnarok he will perish at the hands of Surtr, specifically because the sword is no longer in his possession.

Njord

Njord is the father of Freyr and Freya, and he is a Vanir deity associated with fertility, wealth, and the sea. Considering that seafaring was an important aspect of a Viking's life, it's safe to say that Njord held an important place in the Norsemen's hearts. And yet, one of the only historical accounts that we have of him is the story of how he married Skadi.

Skadi was Thjazi's daughter, who came to Asgard to avenge her father's death at the hands of the Aesir deities (although Thjazi himself was not so innocent, by kidnapping Idun and stealing the gods' immortality). One of her requests was for the gods to make her laugh, which Loki accomplished with his parlor tricks. Another wish of hers was for her father to be honored, and to do so Odin took his eyes and transformed them into stars in the night sky. Lastly, to appease Skadi, she was allowed to choose any god she wanted for marriage with the catch being that she could only choose them based on their feet. Her personal preference was Baldur because he was the most beloved of the gods, and she chose the pair of feet that she believed to be the fairest -worthy only of Baldur. But the gods with the fairest feet ended up to be Njord. Thus the two got married.

Their marriage however was short-lived because they couldn't agree on where to live. Skadi found Njord's home, Noatun (a place near the sea) to be too sunny, and with noisy seabirds that didn't let her sleep. Njord hated the cold of Skadi's home, Thrymheim, and the sounds of the howling wolves. They ended up parting ways after only 18 nights spent together.

Njord seems to have been widely worshipped at some time in the Vikings' history, but we'll never know to what extent or how he was honored by his worshippers.

Chapter 6: Viking Spirituality

Just like all complex religions, Norse spirituality had two main elements: rituals and mystical knowledge that allowed people to understand the inner workings of the universe and how to find their purpose.

When it comes to rituals and other practical ways of worshipping the deities we don't have much to refer to. It is obvious that the Norse gods had a devout religious following which served the social, spiritual, and psychological needs of the Vikings, but the myths and legends do little to explain how the actual worship of the gods played out. Historical evidence speaks of the Norse *blot*, a ceremony through which Odin and other important deities were celebrated. The blots were usually performed at temples or special "blot houses" and they involved sacrifices, of both the human and animal kind. Enemy rulers or noblemen were frequently sacrificed to honor Odin, while animals were used wherever the specific deity had an animal that they could be linked to, such as Freyr with boars. The animals would be killed and consumed by the religious practitioners, in a ceremony that somewhat resembles a modern Christian communion - meaning that the animal was seen as an embodiment of the god.

Blots were a central part of Vikings' lives, and the month of November was named after the divine ceremonies "Blotmonth" or "Bloodmonth." Old Anglo-Saxon writings speak of en masse sacrifices of cattle and horses, where the blood was gathered in special vessels to be consumed and "splashed" over the attendees of the ceremonies. A priest would then bless the meat, vessels, and goblets used at the feast and they would ensure the celebrations. A goblet was ceremoniously emptied to honor certain gods. First Odin, to bless the ruling class, then Freya and Freyr to bring peace and good harvest. Attendees could also empty a goblet to honor their departed.

Viking sacrifices were seen as gifts to the gods, to show appreciation for their blessings and for maintaining order and peace in the cosmos. For the Norsemen, their deities were not perfect or all-powerful. They too were governed by fate and by the laws of the world. Vikings saw them first and foremost as protectors of order, that kept the evil forces in check and seldomly intervened in the events that happened in the mortal world. If we consider how dangerous and harsh the Viking world was, it's not hard to see why the Christian portrayal of a loving and omnipotent god didn't flourish in the minds and hearts of Norsemen. They worshipped their gods with the hopes that they would, in exchange, bless and protect their families and communities. That was all.

Most of the mystic knowledge of the Vikings came from their myths and legends. Through these tales of the realm of the gods and how the cosmos came to be, the Norsemen can easily find ideals,

,oals to strive towards in their

a model for kings, knowledge

fathers alike. Thor is the ultimate

arrior, loyal, and determined to fulfill

to the very end. Freya and Frigg are

is of motherhood, the joy of life, and Norse

gic. Freyr is the personification of wealth,

eace, and prosperity. And the symbolic peace that is established between the Aesir and the Vanir tells Vikings that all the aspects that the deities represent and equally important to lead a happy life and have a successful society. Norse tales are also full of numerology and hidden elements that only the wise and knowledgeable can decipher. These people who were wise enough to see beyond the apparent could practice divination and seidr, to foresee and influence someone's fate.

There's no doubt that Viking spirituality ran deep, and was a lot more complex than Anglo-Saxons of the time believed. And yet, close to the end of the Viking Age, the Norsemen started to give up on

their gods and traditions and emb...
Christianity. There are many dramatized stor...
speaking of forced conversions and even of sain...
or angels that aided Christian clerics in thei...
mission to bring God to the Viking pagans. But in
reality, Christianity came to the Viking world
naturally and progressively. Vikings were very
flexible with their beliefs, and they started to
incorporate Christian elements in their religion as
soon as they set foot on European soil. Sure there
were a few traditionalists who clung on to their
Mjolnir pendants, but most of the Scandinavian
population was open to inclusion, though they
opted to accept one element at a time rather than
make a full 180 degrees conversion. Old Norse
iconography mixed with Christian symbols and
customs to create hybrid religions. It was
perfectly acceptable for baptized Norsemen to
still invoke Thor's protection in their times of
need.

The conversion to Christianity of the Norse
population was slow, and it started way before

Christian missionaries officiated it. The challenge clerics had was not to teach Norsemen the values and practices of Christianity, but rather to convince them to embrace only these Christian elements, and give up on all remnants of their pagan beliefs. The conversion to Christianity didn't happen on its own as a singular event. It came together with the "Europeanization" of Vikings, which led to the Norsemen giving up on traditional values and norms. They made the switch from chieftains to kings, they adopted the Latin alphabet, and little by little the Viking world adhered to European standards.

But what triggered the conversion to Christianity, in the first place? Well, although we can't know for sure, the most plausible reason is the selfish character of the Vikings. Remember, they worshipped their gods in hopes of garnering protection, blessings, and prosperity. But there were things the Norse gods could not provide. Norse deities were ambivalent and not prone to forgive. They did not offer the salvation of one's soul, and they were not always in the "mood" to listen to mere mortals. The Christian God, however, was kind, ever-loving, and forgiving. For the Vikings, all that mattered was who could offer more, thus Christianity was an easy pick. The benefits that it bought were deemed enough to merit worship and loyalty. Viking kings and rulers were usually first to convert because it helped them make powerful alliances. And if the king went first, his people would usually follow. As time went by, Christianity slowly became the default, and the once pagan Vikings became devout followers of God.

Chapter 7: Mythological Creatures

Norse mythology presents a rich and complex world of spiritual and supernatural beings. These beings lived among the gods or humans and carried out their specific roles. The dwarves, for example, are often called upon by the gods for their unmatched talents of crafting incredible weapons and tools. Dragons are fearful beasts that have a special love for material things, especially gold. Such an example is Fafnir, the great dragon that was slain by the Nordic hero Sigurd, to avenge his father's death and obtain the dragon's treasure. Only the most honorable and brave could kill these magnificent and malevolent beasts. And the Valkyries are Odin's familiars and the ones who choose who goes to Valhalla. But there is not much to say of these creatures, at least nothing new or exciting. So, here in this chapter, I'll cover some more elusive sprites of the Norse mythology, some of which will give us a better understanding of the Viking civilization and the values and beliefs they held dear.

Elves

Elves, or *alfar* as they were called by the old Norsemen, were divine beings that were above the human race. They were often described as being tall genderless or androgynous-looking beings, with a pale complexion and light-colored hair. Elves were renowned for their beauty and their ability to use magic, and some stories go as far as to call them gods or demi-gods due to their powers and affiliation with the Norse deities.

As a side note here, we must understand that the way in which the Norsemen classified their mythological creatures was kind of confusing and it left a lot of room for interpretation. For example, there are no clear distinctions between the gods, elves, dwarves, and other beings, and the boundaries between the classifications are blurred further due to the apparently free-handed use of terminology. Some sources describe the Vanir gods as being elves, with Freyir being their lord and ruler, while other texts consider them separate beings. Another result of this confusing classification comes to play when describing the nature of the elves. A long-held belief was that elves were beings of light and goodness, who could heal or aid humans (in exchange for offerings or sacrifices). But in reality, it seems like elves were rather ambivalent, and it wasn't uncommon for them to use their magic to cause illness and misfortune to humankind.

Although this ambivalence was common in Norse belief, Christianity couldn't wrap its head around the concept. So, in an effort to categorize the elven race, 13th-century historians divided them into classes of dark and light elves, drawing inspiration from Christian concepts of angels and demons. *Ijosalfar* were the elves of light, who personified the good attributes of the human race, while the *dokkalfar*, the dark elves, became demonic beings who brought upon temptation and destruction. The distinction went as far as to ascribe a separate realm for each type of elves, with the light elves living in Alfheimr and the dark elves in Svartalfaheimr. It's worth mentioning that these post-Viking Era historians misunderstood many of the Old Norse writings. Such an example of misinterpretation could be the use of the term dokkalfar to refer to the dark-elves. The Vikings used *dokkalfar* when they spoke of the dwarves. Additionally, the realm of the dwarves was called Svartalfar, which is conspicuously similar to Svartalfaheimr, the realm attributed to the evil elves. Thus, the dark-elves of the 13th-century writings may be nothing more than the old Norse dwarves.

In many senses, the early Vikings worshipped elves as they did their deities, in the hopes of winning their blessings. Humans who accomplished great deeds in their lives were believed to become elves after their demise, an element that ties in the worship of elves with that of the ancestors. Perhaps because the elves were somewhat closer to the human realm, so much so that cross-breeding was an option, the worship of elves had ultimately outlived that of the gods, disappearing entirely only when the conversion to Christianity of the Viking world was completed.

Huldra

The Scandinavian space has always had plentiful forested areas, and it comes as no surprise that the dark and mysterious-looking woods sparked the imagination of the old Norsemen. From witches to trolls and shapeshifting monsters, there was no end to what could hide among the trees of Norway, Sweden, and Denmark. Tales of forest spirits are very common in areas with lush greenery, but no spirits are as interesting and treacherous as the Nordic Huldra or Skogstra. These are female spirits who ruled over the vast forest of the Viking world, sowing fear and perhaps curiosity, in men's hearts.

In the early days, forests were seen somewhat as separate realms, that hid both perils and wonders, violence and beauty. It was a place for outcasts and forces of evil, where dangers awaited at every step. And they were not wrong. Without maps or modern navigation equipment, a wrong turn or a slight shift in the weather could lead to someone getting lost, increasing their chances of bumping into dangerous forest beasts such as bears and wolves. Many people who ventured into the forest of the old Norsemen never made it out alive, which is most likely why tales of forest sprites were so popular. They served as explanations of why loved ones failed to return, but also as a warning for children and adventurous youngsters. At the time, blaming natural events such as disappearances on fantastic creatures was more appealing than finding a reasonable and logical explanation. Most mythological creatures are born as a result of this tendency towards fantasizing the "unexplainable."

Our Huldra or Skogsra was a forest spirit who usually took on the form of a young, beautiful maiden with a fox or cow's tail. Because the Scandinavian world was rather big, the creature has many names, and there is a lot of variation when it comes to her descriptions and the stories revolving around her. She would lure young men, make love to them, and then eat them alive, much like the popular tales of the sirens and mermaids who caused shipwrecks and feasted on human flesh. This anthropomorphic being is often portrayed as a stereotypically seductive creature that roams the woods naked and can barely carry her large breasts. Other portrayals of the Huldra describe her as being an animal-human hybrid, that looks beautiful from the front but it has a backside that resembles a rotten tree-trunk. Whatever the version, Huldra is undeniably an anthropomorphic representation of nature itself, that is about alluring and dangerous.

Some tales, however, speak of female forest spirits

that gave birth to half-monster half-human babies, alluding to forbidden relationships between young men and the Huldras. Indeed, not all forest spirit-human interactions led to death and misfortune. Men who willingly became a forest spirit's lover would receive the Huldra's blessings and aid in times of need. A Huldra could ensure that your arrow always reached its mark or that you would survive perilous situations. These relationships would often lead to the human counterparts being looked down upon or even punished by the church. Of course, there were also situations in which the humans would refuse such an intimate relationship, and they could allegedly safely do so by burning the private parts of the spirit. Because most stories of the Huldra and the Skogsra are sexual in nature, they likely have, in part, originated from erotic fantasies of men who spent a lot of time in the woods.

Draugr

Draugr are the undead of the Norse mythology, who would rise from their graves to kill and terrorize the living. These creatures would maintain the physical abilities that they had during their lives, with an added element of magical powers such as the ability to increase their size, superhuman strength, and knowledge of the past and future. Draugr were violent and very hostile towards the living, which is why the Norse people feared them and took many precautions to prevent their dead from coming back to life. One such method was the creation of a special "corpse-door" through which the corpse of the recently deceased was carried to their burial place. You see, the Norsemen believed that the undead could only enter a house by using the door through which their body had last left the house. So they dismantled a part of the walls to use as a "corpse-door," that would quickly be repaired after the funeral was completed. Another way of keeping the dead at bay was to build walls around gravesites, although if the Draugr had the power to grow as tall as they wanted, I don't think that method was too successful. A more strategic approach was to bury the dead with blunt weapons or broken weapons, so the dead couldn't use them or to place a large boulder over a person's grave.

But what caused the dead to come back to life? Norse people, just like other civilizations of the past, had a very deep connection with the afterlife. The fate of the dead was often more important or real for Vikings than their life in the world of the living. Dying an honorable death and being chosen to go by Odin's side was pretty much the goal of a Viking's life. However, death is a complicated concept, and the Norsemen didn't see the bodies of their deceased as being "dead." Reanimation was a real fear, especially because it could happen to anyone. Sure, things like practicing magic, being an outlaw, or being buried outside a graveyard court would make it more likely for the dead to come back to life, but so was dying of an accident. That could happen to anyone, especially in an age and geographic region as dangerous as the Viking one.

Draugr were dangerous creatures that killed any humans they laid eyes upon. But there are also stories and accounts of weird acts done by the undead and specific Draugr that featured in Norse tales. Starting with the first, a quirky thing that the Draugr were said to indulge in was "riding roofs." That means that they would climb on people's roofs at night and stomp on them, to disturb the sleep of the inhabitants. Having a Draugr "riding your roof" was surely preferable to being killed by one, but it was still a way of terrorizing the living. Famous Draugr include Glamr, an extremely aggressive sprite that was killed in a wrestling match by the Norse hero Grettir, and Thorgunna, a Draugr lady who came back to life because the men carrying her to her grave did not treat her body with respect. You'd think that Thorgunna's body was reanimated to get its revenge but you'd be mistaken. In exchange, she came back to cook for them, naked. The men, pleased with Thorgunna's cooking and perhaps impressed with her attire (or lack of) buried her a second time, in a churchyard.

Some Draugr were said to guard the treasure they possessed while they were living, kind of like the nefarious Fafnir who was obsessed with his gold. Apparently, the only correct way of killing a Draugr was by burning it, which is likely part of the reason why ship burials were preferred especially for kings and people of high status - they ensured the dead won't come back while the soul was making its way to Valhalla.

Fossegrim

Fossegrim is a troll or a water spirit that plays the fiddle from beneath waterfalls. This sprite shares many attributes with the Huldra such as its beauty, its alluring nature (the Fossegrim is said to play enchanting music), its apparent nudity, and its ambivalence towards humans. But there is one big difference that sets them apart - the Fossegrim is male. The music of the Fossegrim is said to be so enchanting that even the lame, sick, and old would dance to its tunes. Just as with the Huldra, the Fossegrim is a seductive spirit that can lead humans to their doom. He is more prominent in Norwegian folklore, although legends of the Fossegrim can also be found in Sweden and Denmark.

Some stories speak of women and children who were lured to bodies of water where they ultimately drowned. Again these stories are more likely just ways to rationalize drownings and warn the young ones about the dangers of lakes and rivers. Let's not forget that water is a force of nature, that brings both prosperity through fishing and agriculture but also death for those foolish enough to challenge the depths and currents. The more intimidating and awe-inducing an element was at the time, the more supernatural beings were attributed to it. Our Fossegrim just happens to be one of many such as water serpents and Krakens - the giant octopuses or squids that pulled ships downwards to their demise.

Other stories of the Fossegrim are more lighthearted. It is said that the sprite would teach you how to play the fiddle if you offered him a proper sacrifice. The requirements for the offering were pretty intense. For once, the sacrifice had to be a plump white male goat, offered in secrecy on Thursday evening. The goat had to be thrown into a waterfall, while the animal's head was turned away from the wall of water. Only waterfalls that flowed northwards were considered acceptable. Another type of sacrifice that suited the refined tastes of the Fossegrim was smoked mutton, but this too had a catch - it had to be stolen from a neighbor, on four subsequent Thursdays. If one would successfully make an offering to the water sprite, the Fossegrim would take the person's hand and play the fiddle until their fingers bled. After this harsh training, the person would gain the musical abilities of the spirit. If, however, the goat was too lean or the mutton insufficient in any way, the Fossegrim would only show you how to tune your fiddle.

Because the fiddle was so tightly linked to the legends of the Fossegrim, the instrument was banned from being used in churches, and those who played it were discriminated against in religious communities. This hatred resulted in many fiddles being burnt or destroyed, in an attempt to cast away the esoteric forces.

Kraken

Since I've mentioned the humongous beast, it seems fair to go into a little more detail about this Norse creature that was based on a very real fear of the sea. The Kraken is a species of sea monsters said to swell in the waters of Greenland and

Norway. Many depictions of them describe the Kraken as being so huge that they could easily pass for islands, that, if you were foolish enough to dock for a quick exploration, would sink as soon as you set foot on "land" turning you quite literally into "fish food." This description ties the Kraken to another well-known sea creature, the island whale - a sea beast that was frequently mistaken for land and which took sailors to the depths as soon as they lit a fire on its back. In one way, we can think of the Kraken as the result of humanity's greatest sea-related fears. First, we have the unimaginable size, then the apparently neverending number of limbs and its violent nature. And of course, its preference for dragging ships to the bottom of the sea - a gruesome way to die. We can't really fault the sailors for believing in such stories, especially when they were presented with the perils of the sea on a daily basis.

For people in Medieval times, if you rowed too many miles into the Norwegian Sea, you were merely a few seconds away from becoming the victim of the greatest animal creation that ever existed. The first and foremost sign that you were close to encountering a Kraken was when you started to reel in an unusually large amount of fish. The sailors believed that the fish fled for the surface in an effort to escape the sea-monster, thus resulting in great luck for the fishermen. But escaping the Kraken was not impossible. If the rowers could flee the area in which their catch was suspiciously good fast enough, they could escape with their lives and see from a distance the enormous creature coming to the surface. The Kraken though is not a stupid sea-monster. It was known to form whirlpools with its giant tentacles, to draw in ships, and use small fish as bait for unsuspecting sailors. Nonetheless, many stories make note of the Kraken's appetite for fish and how, if left alone, it wouldn't go out of its way to harm humans. These stories tell the tales of how the creatures used its excrement (which is described in way too much detail as being thick and making the waters appear muddy) to lure fish directly over their mouth for a quick and efficient fish-snack.

I wanted to finish off the Mythological Creatures chapter with the Kraken for two reasons. One would be that it's an extremely popular mythological being that most of us have heard of, at least in passing, and second, it is one of the few fantastic beasts that is based on a real-life animal - the giant squid. These creatures are just as elusive as the mythical Kraken but they are without a doubt real, roaming the waters of the world in search of food and having epic underwater battles with their life-sworn enemies (and natural predators) the sperm whales. With this in mind, it's not hard to understand why so many European legends speak of the Kraken and its formidable nature.

Chapter 8: Ragnarok

In Norse mythology, Ragnarok is the end of the world, kind of like the Christian Apocalypse. It is a great cataclysm that will trigger the destruction of the universe and all its beings, including the gods. For the Vikings, Ragnarok, which roughly translates to "the Fate of the gods" was a prophecy that foretold the doom of all life, and it had a big influence on how the old Norsemen perceived the world around them. Although no one knows when the prophecy will happen, the story itself is very complex and detailed, including signs that foretell the beginning of the end, clear descriptions of the great battle between the gods and the giants, the outcome of the divine war, and what is to come after the apocalypse. Let's go through all of these aspects first and then we'll take the time to understand the impact that Ragnarok had on the Norse civilization.

The Signs of Ragnarok

The first sign included in the tellings of Ragnarok is one that has already happened in the mythological universe of the Norse people, and that is the murder of Baldur. We've covered the circumstances of his death and the deities' attempt to bring him back - for their sake and that of the universe since Baldur's resurrection would have meant the delay of Ragnarok. Then, at some point, the Norns, the three creatures that spin the fate of the cosmos (called Urd, Verdandi, and Skuld) will decree the coming of the *Fimbulwinter* (the Great Winter), a long a bitter winter unlikely any other than the world has seen before. The cold will be so great that the warmth of the sun could no longer reach the Earth, allowing the snow to fall without interruption and the temperatures to drop to unimaginable lows.

This great winter will be as long as three normal winters, with the exception that there will be no summer in between. Mankind will be at the brink of extinction, their desperation to survive chipping away at their morality. At its peak, the frenzy of survival will take control of them all, and the age of swords and axes will begin. No laws of nature or society will be able to stop the chaos of the human world. Fathers will slay their sons, sons will kill their fathers, and brother will turn against brother in hopes of surviving the end times. This situation will only worsen when the two wolves, Skoll and Hati, will finally catch and devour the moon and the sun bringing darkness into the world. The stars too will vanish, leaving behind a black void. Yggdrasill, the great world tree, will tremble, causing the mountains and the trees to fall to the ground.

Then in Jotunheim, the realm of the giants, Fjalar (The All-knower) a red rooster, will warn the frost giants that Ragnarok has come. A second red rooster will announce to Hel and all the dead from Niflheim that the time of the final war is upon the world. And finally, in Asgard, a third red rooster called Gullinkambi, will warn the deities that the giants are coming. The number three, which is used to symbolize the sacred is heavily present in these tellings of the signs of Ragnarok. There are three Norns, Fimbulwinter lasts three winters, and we have three rosters that warn the gods, giants, and dead at the beginning of Ragnarok.

The Great Battle

As Ragnarock starts, all the beasts will run free and join the army of the giants. Fenrir's chain will snap, Loki will escape from his cave of torment, and Jumurgandr, the great serpent, will rise from the depths of the sea, spilling the waters over Midgard. The convulsions created by the coming of Ragnarok will free the ship Naglfar, which is made from the toenails and fingernails of all the dead in Niflehmein. Aboard this ship will be Hel and her dead, the giants, and all the forces of destruction and the captain of Naglfar will be none other than Loki, the god of mischief. With the world now engulfed by waters, the ship will easily make its way to the realm Vigrid, where the last battle will take place. As the great serpent will poison the Earth and the waters with his great venom, Fenrir will roam the Earth, with his jaws wide-open, devouring everything in his path.

While this whole procession will make its way to Vigrid, the sky will open and the fire-giants of Muspelheim will be led by Surtr the destroyer. This procession will march across the Bifrost, breaking the rainbow bridge. Then Heimdall will blow the Gjallarhorn, to announce the beginning of the end. The horn will be heard by Odin's honorable warriors, the *einherjar,* and Freya's *folkvangr*, and they will hurry to march into battle alongside their veneered deities. The fallen Aesir gods, Baldur and Hodr, will come back from the realm of the dead, to join the battle and aid their kin. Odin will consult Mimir's head, for one last time, before deciding to go to battle and fulfill their destiny. They will swiftly arm themselves and then they will follow the All-father, who will lead them to Vigrid, on the back of his trusty steed

Sleipnir. With his spear, Gungnir in his hand, Odin will dive into the battle that he knows he is destined to lose.

The battle of Vigrid will happen as it was foretold. Odin and his warriors will fight valiantly but they will be eaten by the great wolf Fenrir. Vidar, a son of Odin, will avenge his father by holding open the wolf's mouth with one leg in which he'll have a special shoe made only from the leather that has been discarded by shoemakers, and sliding his sword in the beast's throat, killing him in an instant. Garm, the wolf of the underworld, and Tyr will kill each other. Loki will finally get his ultimate punishment by dying at Heimdall's hands, although the guardian deity will also perish in the process. Freyr will be killed by Sutr because he will no longer possess his sword. Thor will finally face his lifelong foe, Jumurgandr, and he will kill the beast with a blow of his precious Mjollin. But the snake's venom will end up putting an end to the mightiest of the Norse gods, and Thor will lie dead on the battleground of

Vigrid after managing to take nine last steps. The number nine here shows Thor's connection to pagan beliefs and signifies the turning point of the battle.

In the end, most of the gods and giants will die, and the dragon Nidhug will feast on the corpses. Other dragons will come and their fire will destroy the world, and the waters will engulf what will be left of it. Thus, a new void will be created, and everything will be as if the universe from before had never existed.

A New World

Many believe that the tale of Ragnarok ends there, but the prophecy goes on to speak of a new beginning. A green and beautiful world will rise from the waters. The gods that will survive Ragnarok, which are Baldur, Hodr, Vidar, Vali, Modi, and Magni, will reinstate the realm of the deities, Ivadoll. Here they will build great houses with golden roofs and they will be ruled by a great unnamed leader. A man and a woman, Lifthrasir and Lif, who were lucky enough to hide in the Wood of Hoddmimir (or in the sacred tree Yggdrasil in some versions) will survive Ragnarok, and they will repopulate the realm of men. A new sun will adorn the skies, and new places will be established such as Okolnir (Never cold) and Namstrod (a shore of corpses). There will also be a new underworld, for murderers and thieves, where the great Nidhug will satiate his hunger for dead meat.

Not much else is known about this new era that will come after Ragnarok.

The Vikings and Ragnarok

The first problem that arises when we look at what Ragnarok meant for the Norse people is the fact that we have two versions of the story. In one, the world ends and all that remains is a void, and in the other one, the demolition of one world leads to the birth of a new one. The generally accepted explanation is that the second version, that in which rebirth follows destruction, is newer and it shows the shift in Norse belief brought by the introduction of Christianity in the Viking world. We can look at this as a representation of the death of the old gods and the birth of a new era, presided over by a mighty ruler, who could or could not be the Christian God.

But let's take a step back and look at the other version, which is more authentic to the Viking way of thinking. In one way, their belief in Ragnarok brought a somewhat tragic meaning to their lives. After all, who wouldn't feel like their life was meaningless if they knew that one day the universe itself will end and nothing and no-one can change or survive that? It is as if you grow up knowing that you are destined to die and disappear forever. However, in another way, the tale of Ragnarok taught Vikings how to act and what was expected of them. It taught them the importance of having a noble attitude and facing your fate with courage and honor. After all, if the gods can courageously march towards their doom and fight valiantly despite knowing that no matter what, they will fail, then so could humans. Thus, Vikings embraced the inevitability of death and focused on accomplishing great deeds and creating a name for themselves - one that would be passed down for all the generations to come.

And their reputation would live on until the arrival of Ragnarok when the world would end.

Conclusion

This marks the end of our Norse journey. We've seen how the Vikings transitioned from a peaceful, agriculture-focused society into a military force to be reckoned with, that made all the European world tremble in fear. But these people were far from our preconceived idea of barbarians, pagans, and mindless brutes. They were an advanced society with a rich culture and deep belief in the sacred and the divine. The Vikings had legal assemblies where they proposed and voted laws for settlements to live by. They were driven, courageous people who were ready to risk their lives for a chance at improving their social and financial situation, and garnering a good reputation. They valued their social bonds deeply and they honored their kin, and even if their ideas of gender roles were still private, the Norse women enjoyed liberties and luxuries that few of their European sisters could dare to dream of in Medieval times.

One of the most important aspects of a Norseman's life was worshiping and honoring their deities, in hopes of winning them over and receiving their blessings. The kings, rulers, and noblemen invoked Odin for guidance and inspiration. The warriors asked for Thor's protection in battle. The farmers celebrated Freya, Freyr, and the mighty Thor to ensure their harvest would be plentiful and that their family will prosper. Although most Norse rituals and traditions are lost to time, we can't deny the deep connection these people felt with their gods. For them, deities were their role models, their guides, their protectors, and the answers to all their questions about life and its purpose.

The Norse also believed in mythological creatures that roamed the forests, waters, gravesites, and the other unseen realms of gods, elves, and giants. Most of these creatures, just as the Norse gods, were ambivalent in nature, able to bring both fortunes and disasters. Their belief in the mythical was so deep that people would take precautions against the living dead and they would banish any individual that seemed to be connected to the esoteric. This negative attitude towards the unexplained was only worsened when the Norse people renounced their faith in favor of Christianity. But that's not the only aspect of the Vikings' life that was changed by the Europeanization of the Scandinavian space.

The shift to Christianity also marks the end of Norse tradition and politics. War chiefs were replaced by kings, the loyal and honorable clans became armies, the trade-cities flourished and the Norse turned their back to their gods. These changes led to military and economic success, but it cost the Vikings their identity. Their pragmatic way of regarding their fate had softened, and even Ragnarok, the grim prophecy of the end of the universe, had changed to better fit this new mentality. It became a tale of hope and new beginnings, a fitting story for the new-generation Vikings, who renounced their old ways as soon as those no longer worked in their favor.

So who were the Vikings? How should we describe this flexible civilization that swept the European world like a storm? They were brave, strong, educated, driven, perhaps greedy, thirsty for adventure, and open-minded. They were warriors, discoverers, poets, story-tellers, and colonists. They took all the opportunities that life threw at them and they never looked back, no matter where their destinies brought them.

I hope you enjoyed our ride through the history, life, and mythological world of the old Norse people. Good luck with your mythological travels and don't forget to keep your eyes open for new discoveries! There is so much that we don't know about these forgotten civilizations and every new archeological finding brings us one step closer to understanding them and finding out who they really were.

Subscribe To Sofia Visconti

As a subscriber you will receive a <u>Free Gift</u> + You wil be the first to hear about new books, articles and more exclusives **<u>just for you</u>**

<u>Click Here</u>

References

Ager, S. (2017). Old Norse language, alphabet and pronunciation. Omniglot.Com. https://omniglot.com/writing/oldnorse.htm

Apel, T. (2019a). Freya. Mythopedia. https://mythopedia.com/norse-mythology/gods/freya/

Apel, T. (2019b). Freyr. Mythopedia. https://mythopedia.com/norse-mythology/gods/freyr/

Ashliman, D. L. (2010, February 17). The Norse Creation Myth. Pitt.Edu. https://www.pitt.edu/~dash/creation.html

Black, J. (2020, June 25). The story of Ragnarok and the Apocalypse. Ancient-Origins.Net; Ancient Origins. https://www.ancient-origins.net/myths-legends/story-ragnarok-and-apocalypse-001352

Encyclopedia Mythica. (2004, October 9). Helgi Hundingsbane | Encyclopedia Mythica. Pantheon.Org. https://pantheon.org/articles/h/hundingsbane.html

Encyclopedia Mythica. (2005, October 11). Helgi Hjörvarðsson | Encyclopedia Mythica. Pantheon.Org. https://pantheon.org/articles/h/hjorvardsson.html

Foster, J. (2020, August 31). Fossegrim and His Fiddle: The Troll at the Heart of Norwegian Music — The American Skald. Jameson Foster. https://www.theamericanskald.com/blog/fossegrim

Groeneveld, E. (2017, November 2). Norse Mythology. Ancient History Encyclopedia; Ancient History Encyclopedia. https://www.ancient.eu/Norse_Mythology/

Harasta, J., & Charles River Editors. (2015a). Decline of the Norse Faith - Odin: The Origins, History and Evolution of the Norse God. Erenow.Net. https://erenow.net/ancient/odin-origins-history-evolution-norse-god/6.php

Harasta, J., & Charles River Editors. (2015b). Legends About Odin - Odin: The Origins, History and Evolution of the Norse God. Erenow.Net. https://erenow.net/ancient/odin-origins-history-evolution-norse-god/3.php

Harasta, J., & Charles River Editors. (2015c). Norse Mysticism and Odin - Odin: The

Origins, History and Evolution of the Norse God. Erenow.Net. https://erenow.net/ancient/odin-origins-history-evolution-norse-god/5.php

Harasta, J., & Charles River Editors. (2015d). Worship of Odin - Odin: The Origins, History and Evolution of the Norse God. Erenow.Net. https://erenow.net/ancient/odin-origins-history-evolution-norse-god/4.php

Joe, J. (1999). Odin Hanging From Yggdrasil (Search For Wisdom) Explained. Timeless Myths. https://www.timelessmyths.com/norse/wisdom.html#:~:text=Odin%20had%20several%20means%20of

Kuusela, T. (2020, July 16). Skogsrå and Huldra: The femme fatale of the Scandinavian forests. #FolkloreThursday. https://folklorethursday.com/folktales/skogsra-and-huldra-the-femme-fatale-of-the-scandinavian-forests/

Lloyd, E. (2020, May 24). Draugr - Vikings Feared This Ugly Living Dead With Prophetic Visions. Ancient Pages. https://www.ancientpages.com/2020/05/24/draugr-vikings-feared-living-dead-with-prophetic-visions/

McCoy, D. (2012a). Baldur. Norse Mythology for Smart People. https://norse-mythology.org/gods-and-creatures/the-aesir-gods-and-goddesses/baldur/

McCoy, D. (2012b). Elves. Norse Mythology for Smart People. https://norse-mythology.org/gods-and-creatures/elves/

McCoy, D. (2012c). Freya. Norse Mythology for Smart People. https://norse-mythology.org/gods-and-creatures/the-vanir-gods-and-goddesses/freya/

McCoy, D. (2012d). Freyr. Norse Mythology for Smart People. https://norse-mythology.org/gods-and-creatures/the-vanir-gods-and-goddesses/freyr/

McCoy, D. (2012e). Frigg. Norse Mythology for Smart People. https://norse-mythology.org/gods-and-creatures/the-aesir-gods-and-goddesses/frigg/

McCoy, D. (2012f). Heimdall. Norse Mythology for Smart People. https://norse-mythology.org/gods-and-creatures/the-aesir-gods-and-goddesses/heimdall/

McCoy, D. (2012g). Hel (Goddess). Norse Mythology for Smart People. https://norse-mythology.org/gods-and-creatures/giants/hel/

McCoy, D. (2012h). Hoenir. Norse Mythology for Smart People. https://norse-mythology.org/hoenir/

McCoy, D. (2012i). Loki. Norse Mythology for Smart People. https://norse-mythology.org/gods-and-creatures/the-aesir-gods-and-goddesses/loki/

McCoy, D. (2012j). Mimir. Norse Mythology for Smart People. https://norse-mythology.org/gods-and-creatures/others/mimir/

McCoy, D. (2012k). Njord. Norse Mythology for Smart People. https://norse-mythology.org/gods-and-creatures/the-vanir-gods-and-goddesses/njord/

McCoy, D. (2012l). Odin. Norse Mythology for Smart People. https://norse-mythology.org/gods-and-creatures/the-aesir-gods-and-goddesses/odin/

McCoy, D. (2012m). Odin's Discovery of the Runes. Norse Mythology for Smart People. https://norse-mythology.org/tales/odins-discovery-of-the-runes/

McCoy, D. (2012n). Ragnarok. Norse Mythology for Smart People. https://norse-mythology.org/tales/ragnarok/

McCoy, D. (2012o). The Aesir Gods and Goddesses. Norse Mythology for Smart People. https://norse-mythology.org/gods-and-creatures/the-aesir-gods-and-goddesses/

McCoy, D. (2012p). The Binding of Fenrir. Norse Mythology for Smart People. https://norse-mythology.org/tales/the-binding-of-fenrir/

McCoy, D. (2012q). The Creation of the Cosmos. Norse Mythology for Smart People. https://norse-mythology.org/tales/norse-creation-myth/

McCoy, D. (2012r). The Creation of Thor's Hammer. Norse Mythology for Smart People. https://norse-mythology.org/tales/loki-and-the-dwarves/#:~:text=Loki%20immediately%20stung%20Brokkr

McCoy, D. (2012s). The Death of Baldur. Norse Mythology for Smart People. https://norse-mythology.org/tales/the-death-of-baldur/

McCoy, D. (2012t). The Fortification of Asgard. Norse Mythology for Smart People. https://norse-mythology.org/tales/the-fortification-of-asgard/

McCoy, D. (2012u). The Kidnapping of Idun. Norse Mythology for Smart People. https://norse-mythology.org/tales/the-kidnapping-of-idun/

McCoy, D. (2012v). The Marriage of Njord and Skadi. Norse Mythology for Smart People.

https://norse-mythology.org/tales/the-marriage-of-njord-and-skadi/

McCoy, D. (2012w). The Mead of Poetry. Norse Mythology for Smart People. https://norse-mythology.org/tales/the-mead-of-poetry/

McCoy, D. (2012x). The Vanir Gods and Goddesses. Norse Mythology for Smart People. https://norse-mythology.org/gods-and-creatures/the-vanir-gods-and-goddesses/

McCoy, D. (2012y). Thor. Norse Mythology for Smart People. https://norse-mythology.org/gods-and-creatures/the-aesir-gods-and-goddesses/thor/

McCoy, D. (2012z). Thor the Transvestite. Norse Mythology for Smart People. https://norse-mythology.org/tales/thor-the-transvestite/

McCoy, D. (2012aa). Tyr. Norse Mythology for Smart People. https://norse-mythology.org/gods-and-creatures/the-aesir-gods-and-goddesses/tyr/

McCoy, D. (2012ab). Ullr. Norse Mythology for Smart People. https://norse-mythology.org/ullr/

McCoy, D. (2012ac). Vanaheim. Norse Mythology for Smart People. https://norse-mythology.org/cosmology/the-nine-worlds/vanaheim/

McCoy, D. (2012ad). Vili and Ve. Norse Mythology for Smart People. https://norse-mythology.org/vili-ve/

McCoy, D. (2012ae). Who Were the Historical Vikings? Norse Mythology for Smart People. https://norse-mythology.org/who-were-the-historical-vikings/

McCoy, D. (2012af). Why Odin is One-Eyed. Norse Mythology for Smart People. https://norse-mythology.org/tales/why-odin-is-one-eyed/

McCoy, D. (2013a). Shamanism. Norse Mythology for Smart People. https://norse-mythology.org/concepts/shamanism/

McCoy, D. (2013b). The Norns. Norse Mythology for Smart People. https://norse-mythology.org/gods-and-creatures/others/the-norns/

McCoy, D. (2013c). The Old Norse Language and How to Learn It. Norse Mythology for Smart People. https://norse-mythology.org/learn-old-norse/

McCoy, D. (2014a). Daily Life in the Viking Age. Norse Mythology for Smart People.

https://norse-mythology.org/daily-life-viking-age/

McCoy, D. (2014b). Odr (god). Norse Mythology for Smart People. https://norse-mythology.org/odr-god/

McCoy, D. (2014c). Viking Clothing and Jewelry. Norse Mythology for Smart People. https://norse-mythology.org/viking-clothing-jewelry/

McCoy, D. (2014d). Viking Gender Roles. Norse Mythology for Smart People. https://norse-mythology.org/viking-gender-roles/

McCoy, D. (2014e). Viking Political Institutions. Norse Mythology for Smart People. https://norse-mythology.org/viking-political-institutions/

McCoy, D. (2017a). The Viking Social Structure. Norse Mythology for Smart People. https://norse-mythology.org/viking-social-structure/

McCoy, D. (2017b). Viking Trade and Commerce. Norse Mythology for Smart People. https://norse-mythology.org/viking-trade-commerce/

McCoy, D. (2018a). The Vikings' Selfish Individualism. Norse Mythology for Smart People. https://norse-mythology.org/the-vikings-selfish-individualism/

McCoy, D. (2018b). Viking Food and Drink. Norse Mythology for Smart People. https://norse-mythology.org/viking-food-drink/

McCoy, D. (2018c). Viking Weapons and Armor (Swords, Axes, Spears, Etc.). Norse Mythology for Smart People. https://norse-mythology.org/viking-weapons-and-armor-swords-axes-spears-etc/

McCoy, D. (2019). The Vikings' Conversion to Christianity. Norse Mythology for Smart People. https://norse-mythology.org/the-vikings-conversion-to-christianity/

McKay, A. (2018, July 19). Creatures in Norse Mythology. Life in Norway. https://www.lifeinnorway.net/creatures-in-norse-mythology/

Mythology Wikia. (2020a, September 25). Fossegrim. Mythology Wiki. https://mythology.wikia.org/wiki/Fossegrim

Mythology Wikia. (2020b, October 26). Sigurðr. Mythology Wiki. https://mythology.wikia.org/wiki/Sigur%C3%B0r

Parker, P. (2018, November 26). A brief history of the Vikings. History Extra; History Extra.

https://www.historyextra.com/period/vik
ing/vikings-history-facts/

Ramirez, J. (2015, August). "Vikings didn't wear
horned helmets," plus 7 more Viking
myths busted. HistoryExtra.
https://www.historyextra.com/period/vik
ing/historical-fact-check-vikings-myths-
busted-did-wear-horned-helmets-violent-
barbarians/

Short, W. R. (2019). Hurstwic Norse Mythology:
The Story of Creation. Hurstwic.Org.
http://www.hurstwic.org/history/articles
/mythology/myths/text/creation.htm

Simon, M. (2014, September 10). Fantastically
Wrong: The Legend of the Kraken, a
Monster That Hunts With Its Own Poop.
Wired.
https://www.wired.com/2014/09/fantast
ically-wrong-legend-of-the-kraken/

Skjalden. (2011a, June 1). Creation of the World
in Norse Mythology. Nordic Culture.
https://skjalden.com/creation-of-the-
world-in-norse-mythology/

Skjalden. (2011b, June 1). Ragnarok - The end of
the World in Norse Mythology. Norse
Mythology. https://norse-
mythology.net/ragnarok-in-norse-
mythology/

Skjalden. (2018, June 15). Important and Secret Numbers in the Icelandic Sagas & Norse mythology. Nordic Culture. https://skjalden.com/important-numbers-norse-mythology/#:~:text=Pagan%20%E2%80%93%20Magic

The Editors of Encyclopaedia Britannica. (1998, July 20). Old Norse language. Encyclopedia Britannica. https://www.britannica.com/topic/Old-Norse-language

The Editors of Encyclopaedia Britannica. (2009, June 4). Fafnir | Norse mythology. Encyclopedia Britannica. https://www.britannica.com/topic/Fafnir

The Editors of Encyclopaedia Britannica. (2019, September 19). Siegfried | Germanic literary hero. Encyclopedia Britannica. https://www.britannica.com/topic/Siegfried

The Editors of Encyclopaedia Britannica. (2020). Ragnarök | Scandinavian mythology. In Encyclopædia Britannica. https://www.britannica.com/event/Ragnarok

The Editors of Encyclopedia Britannica. (2018). Viking | History, Exploration, Facts, & Maps. In Encyclopædia Britannica.

https://www.britannica.com/topic/Viking-people

V.K.N.G. (2019, January 21). 15 Scariest Norse Mythology Creatures [Monster List]. Norse and Viking Mythology [Best Blog] - Vkngjewelry. https://blog.vkngjewelry.com/creatures-of-norse-mythology/

Williams, G. (2016). Ivar the Boneless, Ragnvald of Ed and 6 more Vikings you should know about. HistoryExtra. https://www.historyextra.com/period/viking/8-vikings-you-should-know-about/

Winters, R. (2017, June 30). The Diverse Nature of Elves in Norse Myth: Beings of Light or Darkness? Ancient-Origins.Net; Ancient Origins. https://www.ancient-origins.net/myths-legends-europe/diverse-nature-elves-norse-myth-beings-light-or-darkness-008327

Zarka, E. (2019). Draugr: The Undead Nordic Zombie | Monstrum [YouTube Video]. On YouTube. https://www.youtube.com/watch?v=VNM1Y8i8tuI&ab_channel=Storied